Day Rates, Night Sweats, and Often Barcelona In Between

PAUL KAYAIAN

re-start the Barcelona blog, which encouraged me to finish the book), Ursula Schleuss, Angel and Antonia Bayo, my cousin Jim Bashian, Matasha, Jackie Anastasi, Laura Shahinian, Drew and Denise Torre, George Ketigian, Debra and Stu Duckman, Greg Hourdajian, Chief of Pharmacological Services Kathleen Banksy, Anabel Tejada, Alessandra Menna, Nancy D'Aurizio, Charles and Xanne, Dr. Barry Halejian, Marithe Parra y Arroyo, Joan Roca y Costa, Pedro Bueno, Steve and Karen Guendjoian, Mary Morel, literary power couple Ken Pisani and editrix extraordinaire Amanda Pisani, Greg Herdemian, Moraima, Hussein Alisha, Doug Aprahamian for his invaluable technical shipping and cargo guidance (as well as his ability to lead the Monday Night Basketball fast break like very few others could), Madison Vain for her deeply insightful suggestions and soul-elevating praise, Ivan Anderson's weekly writing classes, and many other faithful readers.

Thank you to Morgan and the team at Book Baby for all their care and feeding of this idea.

Extra special thanks go to Avo, H. Upmann and Montecristo cigars for affording me the pleasure and luxury to smoke and hence, to dream, for forty-five minutes at a time while writing much of these stories and to runway 13/31 at LaGuardia and John F. Kennedy Airports for the moments to imagine faraway places as the planes set up for their final approach directly over my house or crossed the southern horizon in front of me at Jones Beach.

No robots were harmed or A.I. used in the creation of this book.

For more stories about this magical city, do please visit:
https://paulkayaian.substack.com/

Thank you! *Muchas gracias! Moltes gracies!*

Preface

This book is a small effort to leave a tiny trace of my time while on this earth.

It was written at various times in various places via various muses, both real and imagined. A special acknowledgment goes to the city of Barcelona and within it, to "San Pere Mes Alt" street. While living there, it was a cauldron of joy, inspiration and creativity and surely some angst and heartbreak, too: life in and out of balance.

But why Barcelona, you may ask? "Why not?" is my first reply, but I offer this bit of backstory:

"Bar-cel-o-na". An incantation. A prayer. Sometimes a lamentation. A compulsion. An unshakable addiction. Something genetic perhaps, though Ancestry.com did not highlight Spain as it did the Middle East for me. But still, something about this city celestially whispered to me a long time ago that has resonated to the point of deafness. So I embraced it rather than fight it or dismiss it.

I started traveling to Barcelona in advance of the 1992 Olympic Summer Games. The people, the food, the buildings and architecture, the weather, the Mediterranean on your doorstep, all of it added up to incomparable, soul-stirring magic for me. And in a mystical sort of way, I "met myself" there on a Sunday afternoon about 30 years ago.

The city was not only immediately enchanting on my first visit but became increasingly more charming and more dynamic with each return trip. Early on in my travels, I was there over a weekend on a ten-day business trip, so I decided to casually explore it on foot.

In less commercial days, Barcelona was essentially "closed" on Sundays, except for pharmacies and food stores. I wandered through the "Old Town" of *"El Born"* and *"El Gothic"* and stumbled upon a dark, very narrow but intriguing street, "Carrer Petritxol." At one point, you could almost touch both walls simultaneously, it was that narrow. I've been in bad hotel rooms that you could touch both walls – this was much, much better.

No, it did not mysteriously "call" to me, but it was immediately worthy of my right-hand turn down it, with an "ooh, what is THIS place?" vibe. Plaques of hand-painted ceramics that told the history of the street lined the walls, with chocolate shops and antique stores, jewelry, art galleries and a clothing store or two. All were closed, but I wasn't there to shop.

I was completely alone and it was completely silent, not even punctuated by the click-clack of knives and forks on plates for Sunday lunch through an open apartment window. But there just was *something* about that street on that afternoon that kept building with intrigue the further along I went. The hourglass-shaped street opened into a wide courtyard at its end, the "Placa de Pi," in front of a lovely church, with a man quietly playing guitar under an orange tree to seemingly no one but me. No kidding, right then and right there, something "passed" through me (and it wasn't the bad clams I had for lunch): a spirit, of sorts. A bell rang that only I could hear its frequency. It passed through, up, around and settled back in, locked and oscillating to this day.

"...Certain things don't happen often in life. They depend on a conjunction of time and place, on the earthly journey of a certain being and on the dark or conscious impulses that have guided him on that journey. They depend (who knows?) on the stars, on their position in the sky, on the phase of the moon, on the hour in which it arose or will set. They depend on a shadow, a vibration in the atmosphere. They depend on arriving at the right time in the right place. There's a chance in a million - yet it happens. "

(UNKNOWN BATHROOM STALL/FORTUNE COOKIE AUTHOR)

I've been back to Barcelona more than one-hundred times over the years since then, for work and for pleasure (though it was always a pleasure) and to live for periods of time. It has naturally changed and continues to evolve, with pandemics, politics and the Catalan region's fight for independence and autonomy, economic crises, immigration and over-tourism all having left their scars. To balance my excitement before each pleasure trip, I did wonder hard if it was a foolish quest to recapture many very, very happy times that no longer exist, because inevitably, everything changes; because you cannot double-back on a crossed Rubicon. Because maybe Thomas Wolfe *was* right. Because nothing stays the same, although like New York, the taxis there are still black and yellow.

Happily, it remains a magical place for me.

These are a few stories of my time spent in the colossus of tapas.

Paul Kayaian, New York, N.Y. and Barcelona, Spain

Table of Contents

Day Rates,
Night Sweats,
and Often
Barcelona
In Between

The Monday Knights

"YOU'RE NUMBER EIGHT, LET'S GO!"

"Someone make sides already!"

"First four against the second four?"

"I don't care, but we're not getting any younger, fellas, let's go, let's go!

Thankfully, it was another Monday night. Like nearly every other Monday night of our collective lives for the past nearly-forty years, a group of us were at a school gym, playing basketball. Guys had come and gone during various stages of our game, some getting married and being forced into early retirement and some of the younger ones falling away after the school closing summer break, not committed to either the spirit of or need for the game. But the core group had remained intact, and we usually had between nine and eleven players; eight players made the magic minimum number for a "run."

The players were led by "Mike"...because there were three of them: "Big Mike", "Lefty Mike" and "Old Mike". "Big Mike" was big –

six foot two, at least, sweet and good-natured no matter the outcome of the play or brutality of the foul. He always apologized to his teammates for making a bad pass or missing a shot, especially an easy one. I wished that just once I was Big Mike, because I would crush the game like Kareem and shred, terrorize and torment the defense with my size and bulk.

"Old Mike" was the senior statesman, but Old Mike played younger than any of us. He had mastered the art of the offensive rebound and simply played harder and smarter, albeit in shorter stretches, than anyone else. He was also one of the nicest people I ever met.

"Lefty Mike" was the overall best player on the court. Very tough to guard, good shooter, good passer, smart defense, excellent teammate, nice man, funny guy. You always wanted to be on Lefty Mike's team and conversely, dreaded being guarded by him or having to guard him – either way it promised to be a long nine points.

The rest of the group, with some players moving in and out of the general rotation, included "Herb" (due to his preference for marijuana as a pre-game meal and post-game snack), Jazzy (for no obvious reason), The Bear, Cabana John, the Bike Boys and Young Vince (not that there was an "Old Vince" but he was the youngest among our senior set.)

Over the years and the thousands of games we've played together, we've watched each other's kids (and through them, our own passage of time) grow from little tikes who had to be hoisted up near the basket to shoot, to college graduates, and now dentists and lawyers; occasionally, they were even our teammates. We've played indoors and outside, on big courts and now small(er) ones and made the faithful pilgrimage through every snowstorm, traffic jam, flat tire and heat wave to play with and against each other.

We also shared our personal 9/11 tragedies, as half of the original group were firefighters or friends and relatives thereof. The time had also come that we now weep and comfort each other together as, being baby boomers all, our parents begin their inexorable "final approach". We shuddered at the thought of who would be the first grandparent in shorts, sneakers and the Costco-sized bottle of Advil in their gym bag.

Many a business trip has been altered (LaGuardia permitting) and meeting time adjusted, anniversary or birthday celebration deferred to make it on time for our Monday night game. The only thing to keep me away for very long was a two-year posting in London. The first thing I did after getting settled there was find a game to replace, even in some small measure, my Monday night fix. Not exactly a hotbed of basketball in the early 90's, the gym in Chelsea Town Hall was a sea of too-short shorts, pasty white skin, black socks and awful "players" and even the game at the American School in St. John's Wood was a poor replica of the game, much less the unspoken camaraderie we were so fortunate to share. So I hung up my Nike's like a Spanish ham to age until I could get back home rather than hack away in these butcher shops.

"Game is to nine straight, no 'win by two' " we'd tell the occasional guest player, who more often than not was (at least a little) shocked that, invariably older than them, we could still play, blowing past them on fast-breaks and making them work for every shot they took.

By now, we're down to four-on-four on a smaller court; at an average age of, let's say, "fifty-plus." Our legs and lungs, not to mention our knees and backs, couldn't handle more than that. We knew the capabilities and limitations of every player, who could shoot, and who you'd lay off; who hustled and rebounded, and who was generally out of control. Who could go left, or only right. Yet we still played more than most of our nine-points-wins game to final scores of 9-8.

We'd also clearly mellowed with time, replacing the outrage and trash-talking with the post-game "good game" congratulations to each other, akin to the Stanley Cup handshake line. Personally, I think it's a nice but tacit way of saying "thanks for not hurting me" more than any other sentiment, because remarkably, for all the shouting and arguing, energy, frustration, jokes and thousands upon thousands of shots taken, elbows thrown, lies about whether it was out of bounds ("Are you *sure* you didn't touch it last"?) and water-bottle/towel-throwing losses, no one ever really, truly got hurt.

Until last Monday.

Lefty Mike certainly seemed fine during warm-ups. We talked and joked about the usual things: work, wives, the Mets. But with the score eight to five, Lefty Mike was suddenly on the bench, turning whiter than public school chalk.

"Mike? The game isn't over. It's only eight-five. Mike!"

"Mike! Mike, you okay?" Turns out, he wasn't, but we wouldn't know how badly for another forty minutes.

The initial "I'm fine, really" macho-posturing quickly became a group confession of "Hey, we're almost sixty now, boys, we can't fool around with this".

You learn quite a bit about people you seemingly know for so long when a) you travel with them and b) when a kind of panic sets in. That panic can be anything from choking on a piece of hotdog at a backyard barbeque to trouble in a bar with some young guns who see the old guys as easy pigeons. Many a "man" has slipped out of his Superman cape and then the back door of the bar when faced with certain situations, and conversely, guys you never would think to be bold, charged into the fray.

The first reactions were a comical, disorganized mix of "Get some orange juice" to "Boil water"! "He's not diabetic, you idiot, just give him some water and back off the guy!" One calm fellow offered two aspirins and together, after no obvious improvement in his color or general response, and with no CPR-trained firemen playing that night, we convinced him (and each other) to go to the hospital, quickly forming a hazard-lights-flashing convoy. He said only that he was light-headed, but there was clearly something wrong. And if he went down, we all went down. Such is the brotherhood of the hardwood.

We piled into Booth Memorial Hospital (now it's called "NY Hospital Medical Center of Queens", but I also still call it "Shea Stadium", okay?) and after dousing ourselves with a bucket of Purell, we grabbed a spare wheelchair for Mike. While Lefty Mike was not having the Fred Sanford-style "Elizabeth-this-is-the-big-one" type of chest-clutching pain, he *was* slumping in the wheelchair and clearly beginning to fade. We pushed our way to head of the triage line.

Whisked into the emergency room, he immediately failed his EKG test and was, in less than a twenty-four second shot clock violation, deep inside the underbelly of the ER. The nurse came out to tell us shortly thereafter that he was having a heart attack, with one artery completely blocked. Suddenly, ten doctors and nurses descended upon him, with consent forms and gauze pads boxing each other out for position. One doctor said "I know it looks like chaos, but we really do know what we're doing here". And they did. Twenty-three minutes later, the stents were being inserted, the colour came rushing back to red Irish face and he, amazingly, went home two and a half days later.

Over the wailing objections of his wife and the silent panic of our own realizations that it could have been anyone of us as easily as it was Lefty Mike, the doctor said that with rest, medication and a change in diet, he would be back on the court by September. "Playing basketball actually saved his life. This would have happened much sooner, and would have been a lot worse, had he not had the both the regular exercise and the quick-thinking care of his teammates. You guys saved his life".

Basketball saved his life; his teammates simply got the assist. I wonder if that doctor knows how to go to his right? We might only have seven guys until Lefty Mike comes back.

Moroccan Cab Ride

I JUMPED INTO THE CAB in front of "2 Bros. Pizza" ("a buck a slice") and before I could even give the driver my destination, instantaneously, like having a hood thrown over me and being beaten with a blunt object; like popping my forehead and saying "I could've had a V-8!"; like fresh bread or a gas leak or your kids socks, I was hit by a blast of perfume. No, it definitely was *not* the usual olfactory effect when getting into a taxi in New York, which made for a very welcome and disorienting surprise.

I was instantly lost. Not the taxi, but me: sucker-punched by "her" teasing, elegant scent, I was time-warp transported to the embrace of a woman who clearly had *just* gotten out of the cab, her perfume trailing behind the bullet-proof partition. I just sat, apparently, and took in the smell, my mind racing with a slideshow of images: Did she have a hat? Was she obese? Was the seat, still warm from her ass, shapely or misshapen as it were? Was she dressed elegantly or was this her only attempt at cleaning up?

I pictured the object of Pepe Le Pew's affection atomizing herself before he made his move, a cloud of sandalwood and citrus, bergamot and botanicals choking the space behind the driver's glass. After a moment or three, I realized that we had not moved. So did the cabdriver, who smiled in the rear-view mirror, and gurgled a "Hello my friend" as he waited for me to tell him my destination.

I snapped out of my stupor and said "oh, right, um, Thirteenth and Fifth please," and off we went. But I was still mesmerized, captivated by the scent and the immediacy of her presence there and implored the cabbie for details.

"Who was just here? Just now, who was it? Tell me about her" I implored.

"I'm sorry?" he questioned, and by the second syllable, I knew he was Moroccan. "Who was just here?" I asked? Was she beautiful? Was she young or old, big or petite?"

We laughed, but I was arrested by the possibilities. Each answer he gave was like another stroke of a courtroom charcoal sketch. "No, not fat, definitely not."

"Was she pretty? Beautiful, even? Was she younger than forty? I think she must have been," I said, before he could even answer.

"Yes, young. Of course, I have to drive, so I could not actually take long look at her, but yes, young. Young girl, no, no, young woman".

"Where was she going? Where did you take her", I begged. "Was she going home? To a bar? A party? Was she alone?"

"Home I think. Yes, it was an apartment building. But perhaps she was not going to her home, but to the home of another?" Hmm yes, "another". *An other*. A paramour unworthy of such style, such attention to detail. She was sure to be disappointed by the end of the night, all dressed to kill, only to be crushed by another loser guy.

It was only six p.m. on a Monday and this was *not* Monday perfume. Six p.m. was what the French call *"l'heure bleue"* the space in time when you look back on the events of the day and look forward to the night ahead. A time they consider a romantic combination of reflection, confusion and mystery.

"Pretty woman, yes. Very pretty woman" he confirmed.

By Twenty-Seventh and Seventh, the scent had largely faded, by way of the window edge cracked open to dehumidify the backseat on a rainy night and by the scented imbalance provided by Mohammed's dinner on the front seat, a tuna sandwich with liberal splashes of harissa sauce.

"Habibi", I asked, What do you think of Syria these days? Do you see what is happening there?"

"Crazy! Very crazy! But it's good for Morocco!"

"Good? Really? Why? Aren't you worried you are the next domino? That ISIS will come to Morocco's door and kick it in? Isn't Hassan worried?"

"No, no, no more King Hassan, now it King Mohammed VI. Yes, ISIS quite possible yes, but for us, for Morocco, all is good. We say to the peoples, come to Morocco, come, now is a good time. It is safe, and we have a king."

"It's what we say to each other, too: we are poor, we have nothing, but at least we have a king!"

The intoxicating scent of that perfume was now long gone, but it attracted two other unintended people that night.

"My friend, that will be $13.70."

It was the happiest twenty dollars I'd spent in a long time.

Mr. Molina and the Olive Oil Sisters

I MOVED IN ACROSS THE STREET, Carrer De San Pere Mes Alt, from Mr. Molina a few months ago. In the narrow, alley-like passages of the district called Ciutat Vella (or "old city" in the Catalan language) of Barcelona, you were quite close to the neighbors across the way. Built loooong before air conditioning and designed to give relief from the relentless sunlight, the streets and hence the apartments that lined the streets were often cool and dark. The sunshine made contact with the tiled passages and came through the windows of your apartment for only about the length of time it took to have a *cortado* coffee and a *churro*, then it was back to the cool shade as the sun continued its rotation.

Despite the proximity, there was always a respectful, tacit "no peeking" rule, which, as I learned, extended to the casual toplessness at the beach, too. Presumably, people did not peek into my apartment either, though there was little to see. Yet without peeking I could not help but "feel" their presence, silently acknowledging the rhythmic click-clack of the knives and forks and glasses at each mealtime through their open windows. The conversations were often muffled or muted by the sound of bad TV show laugh tracks, cackling to jokes in a language I did not yet fully understand.

I admit, in the early days of my move to Barcelona, where I was on a six-month contract teaching English *("You Talking to Me? Learn English with a Real New Yorker")* and before I learned of the no-peeking rule, I peeked discreetly, but peek I did. I gazed and imagined and wondered and dreamt about the lives of all the people that I could see and hear from my apartment window. I embraced their windowsill plants and yes, the XL-sized pantaloons on the old folks' clotheslines; the garlic-soaked smells and that hypnotic bing-bong-bing sound of the ambulance sirens of Barcelona, all notes of the soundtrack of the city. I took it all in through my open window.

I had the good fortune to have an apartment with front and rear views – the living room overlooked Carrer De San Pere Mes Alt and the kitchen, terrace and bedroom looked into the courtyard that encompassed seven other buildings of differing heights, configurations and ages, from modern to crumbling, all of which overlooked a spectacular secret garden in the center.

At the street level of my apartment was "All i Oli" a shop specializing in all kinds of olive oil and garlic, owned by two sisters, Almudena (the "A") and Oracion (the "O"). They were both very nice, always warm and welcoming with smiles and waves (but never a discount!). They were like block captains, watching the street like hawks and following the lives of all those around them. They were veritable fonts of information – you wanted to know something about the street, a shopkeeper, a shady character or any kind of history of the block, you dipped your finger in the sister's knowledge and they anointed your brain. They lived in the back of the shop and one afternoon soon after moving in, gave me the lowdown on the street and its characters, who you could trust (them!) and who to avoid (the fruit seller with the outdated milk further down the street). They had invited me in for a neighborly coffee, and to grill *me* on who I was and what I was all about. That was where I learned about Mr. Molina, who had befriended them years ago after he expertly repaired their mothers' treasured antique wristwatch.

I could see Mr. Molina from across the way at an angle from my kitchen window to his, sitting at his table, eating his breakfast or dinner, usually watching soccer, though I am not convinced he was really watching at all, but just appreciating another voice in the room. I secretly called him Mr. Molina to give some shape and form, adding a bit of familiarity to my new surroundings where I didn't know anyone. I referred to him as my neighbor, maybe even as my friend, though only in my head.

He always ate in front of a little TV, that blue glow bouncing off both the Spanish tiled floor and Bialetti coffeepot and always with a small tumbler of red wine on the table, too. Sometimes his cat darted in and out and would put two paws up on the windowsill to catch a breeze or simply view the world outside of the apartment.

At the end of both good days and bad days, lonely days and thrilling days, I took comfort in the simple check-in, the peek across the courtyard that Mr. Molina unknowingly provided to me. That I could secretly and privately count on his nightly routine as a re-set of my world back to normal, while still getting used to life here, was a sweet singular moment of happiness for me.

Occasionally, for a kind of dessert, Mr. Molina would lean out of his windowsill in a classic forearms-on-an-old-pillow way, and have a small cigar, dreaming and looking out over the street below. I concluded Mr. Molina lived alone – no wife, no kids, no grandkids, and no girlfriend. Just alone with his TV, his cat, his tumbler of red wine and the occasional small cigar, which put him in my highest esteem.

I had come to love cigars after having the good fortune to travel throughout much of Europe for business and came to see them as a sweet coda to a productive business meal with clients. On top of the inherent pleasure of a cigar, smoking a cigar also re-positioned me with clients as "one of them" and not "the American". I ate and drank what they recommended and afterward, kicked back after what was always a sensational meal with a good cigar. It made them happy, made me even happier and made the deal-making even sweeter. So with the freedom and public acceptance, at the end of my day, I would often walk the streets with a cigar, incredibly grateful for the tobacco culture of Spain (and not wanting to stink up my apartment, either) and take "*el paseo*" or "the stroll" after dinner to digest.

Mr. Molina was a simple man who grew to live simply from a quiet and simple boyhood. His parents were also quiet and simple and hence, he had no brothers or sisters – more than one child might have been too complicated for Mr. Molina's parents, even if it might have made for more fun for Mr. Molina.

His parents led a hard Catholic life – penitent, observant, unyielding and unquestioning. True to God's word, they were never led into temptation and never really allowed Mr. Molina to stray from the straight and narrow, in either thought or word or deed. They unfortunately did let slip, in the briefest moment of emotion while he was asking about family things for a school project, how he was conceived by mistake. The reality of this illumination was not divine and haunted Mr. Molina for his entire life.

There were also the undeniable-though-painfully-rare moments of secret tenderness between Mr. Molina and his mother: the occasional candy treat when they had to go shopping, complete with the stern admonition not to tell his father; the occasional trip to the park for a walk and hop-skip-jump on real grass when the tailor shop was slow and his mother had some free time; the times when his mother rubbed his head or back when he had a cold or felt, *he* felt, too ill to go to school – his father always disagreed and he went to school. No matter what. Those feelings were exacerbated when he was sent to live with his terrible aunt and uncle for almost a year during an especially difficult time for his parents. He felt it was his fault that they could not manage each other much less him, too. The guilt of his unplanned and unwanted presence weighed heavily on Mr. Molina throughout his childhood, yet he ached, how he ached for his mother during those days away from his joyless home: the smell of her close to him in a hug so rare and often chilly, even if he did not understand what love was, with so little of it in his life.

He did have a cat, briefly, which he enjoyed. To be clear, he didn't actually *have* a cat – the care and feeding of a pet were not in the Molina family hymnal. He often saw the same cat in the neighborhood and would play with it and pet it gently. Under the circumstances, with no one to tell him otherwise, he decided it was "his cat" and named him "Athos" after the dark, simple, quiet and brooding Musketeer. He also told himself he would have a cat of his very own someday when he was of an age that no one could say no to him.

With the absence of close friends or parents who encouraged joy or fun, Mr. Molina logically and thankfully loved to read and quietly dream in his simple bedroom about a not-so-simple life. Maybe even that of a Musketeer! He often imagined he was Athos, the Musketeer who had abandoned his aristocratic and lavish lifestyle after the mysterious death of his wife. Mr. Molina understood Athos, past and present: a man who usually keeps quiet and stays in a dark, somber mood to help hide his past pain. Mr. Molina accepted his own quiet life. But privately? He did not accept it so gracefully or humbly and longed for the life of a Musketeer, like any boy would, or really any life different from his. He ached for a "hero's journey" as he understood and enjoyed reading mythology: to leave known and conventional safety in life and take on a complete spiritual and psychological change of and within himself. Swords swinging against wild beasts! Fair maidens and distressed damsels on his arm! The triumphant return to a liberated city and adoring crowds!

But those journeys were tests of human capacity, knowledge, perseverance and courage. Athos was *his* hero. But while Mr. Molina knew, or at least felt he had the perseverance to achieve something he also knew, deeply and painfully, that he would never have the courage to advance his dreams beyond the rooftop of his apartment. He would never be a hero because he knew he did not have the courage to transform his way of thinking and ultimately, of being.

Within these dreams of transformation, Mr. Molina also dreamed about a wife and what she might be like, knowing not-so-deep down that he would never actually have one, or even have a girlfriend.

It's not that he didn't want a wife, not at all, but the thought would have to be enough for Mr. Molina because he feared the reality of his total failure if he even considered trying to participate in the process of love.

Nonetheless, the quiet life worked for him, or maybe he just acquiesced to what he feared (and was reminded by his parents) was his foregone destiny: live it and learn to like it. Love was not a word or an emotion used in Mr. Molina's home very often. Maybe even less than often. It wasn't painful, but it was empty.

Mr. Molina's father was a tram car driver, which suited him well: "go straight" was the rule of the job, not too fast and not too slow. Just stare straight ahead, all day, every day and talk to pretty much no one. His mother was a seamstress, sewing beautiful clothes she would never dream of wearing much less owning, for rich people she would never know, going places she would never have been invited to. She kept her head down and sewed, all day, every day.

Mr. Molina was never really encouraged to explore or to try or to test the boundaries that defined him, enveloped him and quietly suffocated him. That made his life, and the pleasures or lack thereof, also quite simple. Their family vacation was a day, maybe two, at the beach, with a picnic, and the prize for being a good boy was a soda. Sitting quietly with his parents. That was "fun" he was told. I suppose you could call it "pleasant", a word without emotion, and certainly devoid of joy.

He had some friends in school, casual and nice but wholly superficial – no one who he would run into after many years and greet or be greeted with back slaps of delight and fond remembrances. He was bullied a bit but usually only when there was no one else to bully that day. Keeping a low profile was fine with him for many reasons, avoiding bullying being one of them. He was not here, or there, to bother anyone nor have anyone bother him. He was fine with quiet anonymity. Mostly.

But he ached inside. How he ached inside.

To be sure, like all of us, he had hopes and aspirations for a life greater than his present one, or that of his parents. But Mr. Molina decided that the life of safety modeled by his parents was good and noble and worth the sacrifice of never stepping out onto the limbs of life, much less jumping from them, to see what it felt like to freefall or better yet, to fly. It was a struggle during his teens, naturally and biologically, but he pushed on by pushing down, supported only occasionally by the clothesline of Sra. Torres across the way, whose shameless display of her lingerie let Mr. Molina dream for hours as the wind gently caressed her drying unmentionables. Of that, or much else, did he dare not mention a word to anyone. It was this lack of friend, confidante or confessional that ate Mr. Molina up inside. Loneliness was often his only companion.

He knew, he felt, he imagined and maybe even was suffused with the idea at the dinner table by his parents that his life was destined for quiet work. Perhaps some kind "bench work" they told him (they didn't *suggest*, or wonder aloud about such things – they told): shoemaker. Or perhaps a maker of violins or other musical instruments that took time and care, patience and quiet attention, without meetings or bosses or customer demands interrupting him and his focus. This is what they thought of him and his capabilities and potential in life. Noble? Sure, but clearly his dreams were pre-limited for him.

He turned out to be a watch maker and repairer – which was befitting as it was a slow, steady, wordless and careful process - and a good one at that. But it also reminded him, twenty-four hours each day, what time it was in the passing of *his* days. Alone. Down to the very minute.

I would see saw Mr. Molina at the market buying jamon or fish (always the cheaper cuts); in the *farmacia*; the *forn de pa* and discreetly through my kitchen window into his. I would also sometimes see him and Athos on the roof of his building across Carrer De San Pere

Mes Alt on nights when I wanted a cigar but didn't feel like walking, flying his kite. While up there, he often fed the birds, the pigeons and the seagulls with their crazy, haunting cries. I imagined that he saw them as his "friends" and were always happy to see him, as friends are, despite dropping their happy tidings all over the roof and occasionally dive-bombing the street below when they took off for the day or returned en masse for their dinner reunion and breadcrumb supper from Mr. Molina's hands.

Through it all, I went about my day, teaching, and preparing lessons plans; shopping; taking long walks on the weekends and peeking, just peeking, across the street at the scene below and across the hall, smiling to myself when I caught Mr. Molina, like clockwork, at his kitchen table with the TV on, cat on the windowsill and a tumbler of red wine by his hand.

Nothing in life stays the same; for better or for worse, nothing stays the same. Players get traded from your favorite team. TV shows get cancelled. The little bakery that sold the most delicious things closed because they raised the rent.

So it is, but, I thought, should not have been with Mr. Molina. A watchmaker kept time, and a schedule, didn't he? It seemed so. So when he was not in the kitchen at the generally appointed hour, at first I gave it no mind. I mean, he must have other things to do, right? A last-minute repair? A watch with a complicated complication? Maybe, just maybe, Mr. Molina had gone to the movies?

And yet, his kitchen was dark again two nights later. Odd, I thought, at a minimum. Uh oh, I thought, as my mind expanded the maximum possibilities of the reason for his dark kitchen.

I felt strangely connected to Mr. Molina, though I never met him directly. Like the pigeons and the seagulls, I thought of him as "my friend" across the way. Like him, I sat alone at my kitchen table: one glass, one plate, one bowl, one knife, one fork and one spoon. I did, though, allow myself wine in a proper wine glass, even if it was from Ikea.

Was my friend in trouble of some kind? Had he gotten sick and if so, who would take care of him? Could it be he was on an actual vacation, the kind of which he never had before? No, I could not picture Mr. Molina with a little suitcase, fedora and suntan lotion packed along with his Bermuda shorts. Had he finally gone off to fight dragons and rescue fair maidens from their peril, taking them into his arms and riding off into the countryside? Yea, um, no. No way.

Then finally one night, after nine straight nights in "The Disappearing Act of Mr. Molina" I saw the glint from his watch. It reflected the shine off the streetlight shaped like a king's crown outside our windows as he sat in the darkness of his kitchen. Though the setting has changed, he was back! After sighing with an odd sense of relief, I found out what happened the next day from one of the All i Oli sisters. They told me that his cat Athos had died. They say cats have nine lives: Athos, sadly, only had eight.

I lived on the third floor and one breezy night, returning after a cigar *paseo*, felt a chilly wind sweeping down the stairs. Hmm, odd, I thought, it's usually like a monastery in the hallway, with the unique European timed light switch on the wall that gave you *just* enough time and light to climb the stairs and get inside your door. But then I heard a "clang-clang-thump" and went to see what was up.

The door to the roof was open. It didn't seem to be pried open or tampered with, but it was open nonetheless. As I stepped over the saddle to see what or who was out there, I was met with a simply stunning view.

Red clay rooftops? Check. Satellite dishes everywhere? Check. Clotheslines airing out the underwear of Catalunya? Check.

In June, the sun stays out in Barcelona until 10 p.m. not 8:30 like in New York on our best pre-solstice night, but fully till 10 pm. It's remarkable and simply beautiful. It captured the whole Mediterranean lifestyle thing for me in an instant: the ocher colored buildings, healthy food, average daily temperature and endless proximity to and views of the sea, among other sybaritic regional pleasures.

But it was particularly spectacular because of the *clarity* of the sky, as it eased towards sundown. Clear as clear could possibly be with a sky so blue! Bluer than the *"calas"* of the Costa Brava. Bluer than a newborn baby's eyes. So blue I felt that I could reach up to the sky with my finger and the blue would come off onto it like oil paint, coating my nail and leaving a tear in the horizon.

Like a long, lingering kiss, blue sky eventually gave way to the oncoming night of white stars on a black velvet drape. But it passed through a Roy-G-Biv state, going from blue to the shade of pink on the label of a bottle of Evian water, slowly, slowly melting, and rotating over us as if we were in a planetarium watching it all unfold.

The air was fresh and I felt that I could see the curvature of the earth beyond the Mediterranean Sea in front of me. I don't know much about astronomy or the planets or things of that nature, maybe just enough to fool some of the people all of the time, but when I draw a blue-sky stained finger across the latitudinal divide between NYC and Barcelona, the two don't seem to be too far off-line. So I'm not sure why we only stay light until 8:30 and Barcelona stays light until 10 p.m., but I was so glad to be in the 10 pm place instead of the 8:30 place.

As I finally snapped out of my stunned amazement, having been nearly frozen in place by the warm sun and scene before me, I heard a kind of snapping, flapping sound. It wasn't someone's laundry, but some other kind of whistling sort of sound I "knew" but could not place. When I focused, I also turned a bit so I could "see" where the sound was coming from.

There on the opposite rooftop, in the fading light of a perfect Mediterranean sunset, stood Mr. Molina, flying a kite. He seemed to be at peace with himself. He seemed to be at peace with Athos' passing. Athos was the one thing he loved that also loved him back for exactly who he was.

There he was, all by himself. With a small tumbler of red wine perched on the ledge and a little cigar tucked into the corner of his smile.

And all was well again on Carrer De San Pere Mes Alt.

Everyone Else
(Is Wrong...)

EVERYONE ELSE GETS ON THE WRONG line in front of me. Everyone else has more than twelve items at the supermarket, or pays by check, or can't find their CVS card to get their fucking ten-foot long printout of useless coupons after they pay.

While we wait.

The card, by the way, is on their stupid keychain, the one that has the Lucite-covered picture of their dog, with sixty-two other shoppers' chips and eighteen keys and takes the cashier forever to angle *that* chip in front of the card scanner. After three unsuccessful, register-cursing, scanner-scratching tries they then have to slowly type the damn number in.

While we wait. No, really, we will all just wait.

Everyone else falls into a trance at the red light, checking their stupid phone for non-existent messages. I see them, as I am inevitably right behind them, watching them drift into the traffic ether while I count 1…1.5 as my hand approaches the horn and my eyes roll into my head…2…horn, blasting them back from their stupor. At least I get two seconds of joy from their startled semi-embarrassment.

Everyone else stands in the middle of the sidewalk on a busy street. It's selfish, just flat out selfish, stopping as if *no one* is also walking there and might have to walk around them, instead of standing off to the side. So, walk around me, they think. Hey, you selfish fuck, step aside, I think. They are just like everyone else.

Everyone else *never* knows what they want when they get to the register at a take-out counter. Everyone else never stops looking at their phone long enough while on line to look at the damn menu board, step forward and order. Neat, simple, quick, but *never*. They stare, then "Hmmm" and hem and shuffle and finally ask,"Uummm, can I getta?" "Lemme getta?" How long an order are you placing that you could not memorize "…Lemme get some chicken fingers and a Coke…" "Yea and some fries, too!" two people back? No, really, we'll just wait. No, go ahead, take your time.

Really.

We'll just wait along with everyone else.

Modern Love

(Some tips on how to find the man of your dreams online…or at least have a date that doesn't suck)

> *Women dangle the promise of sex in the hope of finding love…*
> *Men dangle the promise of love in the hope of having sex… Sometimes,*
> *but only sometimes, both get what they want….*

(BATHROOM STALL PHILOSOPHER)

SWEET MYSTERY OF LIFE…. YOU are (still) the dream of many men and yet you are still alone and looking for "me" (or a reasonable facsimile of me) here. As a gender, we have disappointed you, generally, and bored you, mostly, and confused, offended, occasionally harassed and overall left you hungry for even a crumb of sanity and decency. Yet, we remain somewhat indispensable to you and hence, often fruitlessly, you continue to search for one, if not "the" one, looking for the magical pin-stick from that shiny needle in this otherwise filthy, damp, rank, and depraved stack o' hay called "online dating".

Not everyone, of course, has hit their personal jackpot, but a recent Pew Research Center survey said 12 percent of Americans have married or been in a committed relationship with someone they met online, while 57 percent of those who had tried a dating app said their experience was somewhat, if not very, positive. That leaves almost half of America home alone with a glass of wine and the remote control. The study did not say how good or bad the date actually was – feel free to fill in the blank there. The same study also suggested online dating was a "…good way to meet people…" with a 60 percent "approval" rating.

Your results may have varied.

You know the unmatched power of a kiss and wish, desperately, to be beaten to the surrender point at the kissing game, but few, maybe two at most in your life, kissed you with any authority or command, with any talent or understanding of the link between your lips and the strength of your knees. You persevere, despite the exhausting routine of swiping, clicking, anticipating, wondering and eye-rolling because hope is a powerful addiction and loneliness is one tough screeching monkey to shake off your back. Also, because it's better than reaching for that pint of soy kale chip frozen dessert-like concoction and emptying it in less time that one episode of "The Bachelor".

Your body still works – with all that yoga and all those yoga pants, it better, dammit! So does your brain - you pronounce (almost) every word you use correctly and you use your words with both flair and care. The word "whatever" is not in your lexicon, but "lexicon" is. You wish, *so* wish, you did not have to be on four different online dating sites, but you are, hoping to flood the end zone and catch what is becoming a Hail Mary pass. (Hey, I'm a guy, and hence the need to use a sports metaphor). But despite eight million potential lovers all around you, your mirror-image has been a cracked and fogged apparition.

Apparently, based on the pleading bleating's I read from many of your profiles, we men (and I accurately generalize here) present a preponderance of shirtless Cro-Magnon pictures holding fish or some other freshly killed dinner offering, paired with a grunted "Hey." "What's up?" or "You're hot!" whisper of our most tender affection. Compelling, indeed.

We also seem to contact you from places requiring a passport, a stay of execution and/or tetanus shots. This I cannot explain beyond the international phenomenon of loneliness. Or the global fascination with Barbie.

Ladies, I am not Cupid. I have neither bow nor arrow, but perhaps I can help optimize your search nonetheless.

While I cannot offer a bullet-proof inbox to deflect this lot, hopefully the following suggestions will act as both bear-spray and intoxicating perfume, to turn *your* online profile into a sirens call, leaving us drooling, wide-eyed and strolling on the beach (or cuddled on the couch) with you, the only dead fish near us being the cracked carcasses of the lobster (with champagne!) dinner we've just had.

So, here goes:

1. No more pictures of you with better-looking girlfriends. Yes, apparently men favor the witness protection look of baseball cap and sunglasses in a grainy, outdated photo. Again, I do not condone or make excuses – we *are* a sorry sack.

But, with that, I think I'd rather see *you* holding a fish than smiling next to your often much-sexier friend at a birthday party and me trying to figure out how to connect with her. The same goes for pictures *not* of you, like sunsets, autumn leaves, unrecognizable skylines, multiple pet shots or even you with your dear old dad. "Mr. Baxter", your Lhasa Apso *is* cute. I guess. But we do not want competition for your affection or the space on the couch next to you, especially if we have to walk behind it with a blue NY Times delivery plastic bag. In the rain. That's not the threesome we have envisioned.

2. Acknowledging our collectively poor taste in photo's, often in front of cars, boats and private jets we do not own and including the ubiquitous selfie-in-the-bathroom-with-all-our-meds-and-Minoxidil-clearly in the background, once again, please show *us* the "right" way and pick normal pictures for your profile. Simple pictures. Sane pictures, not Halloween make-up shots; Santa-hat-at-the-company-Christmas-party; where-the -heck-is-my-Xanax look in your eyes or the same pose of your good side for eight straight pictures. We got it after the 3rd one that you look better on your left side than right and will position ourselves accordingly. Thanks for the heads up.

3. When you do post pictures, we really do not need the travelogue captions. Whether you were in Mumbai, Dubai, Shanghai or Bed-Stuy, none of this information will draw our hearts closer to you, except if we are airline pilots or travel agents.

4. Hey, Namaste *this*: *one* yoga pose. Please!

5. If you are a "work in progress", let us know when the job is finished, preferably on time and under budget.

6. Ninety-nine and forty-four hundredths of us *swear* we will never call you and ask you to switch from a T-shirt and jeans into a little black dress for a White House state dinner in fifteen minutes flat. It's an admirable skill, without question, but the likelihood of needing to pull this presto-change-o trick out of your life's toolbox is equal to the Chicago Cubs winning the World Series (*again*). Good to know though, thanks!

7. You are "...happy, fun, positive, at a great place in life...." Yea, so are we, so why are we here, exactly, if things are going so swimmingly? Um, because we are none of the above, or at least not enough of the above to have made our last relationship(s) last. Good that we are all these things, though. Because really, who wants to curl up on the couch, or clean up the Friday-night-with-Netflix popcorn pieces that fell between the cushions, with a crank pot?

I hope this helps. I hope you find true love and quickly close all your accounts and tell the story to your new family and friends with a smile on both your faces about how you two met.

And if you promise to go fishing with him, even once, or let him go fishing more than once, he will promise to make a fire in the unused fireplace and cuddle with you on the couch, maybe even more than once.

See, sometimes you both get what you want.

A List Of Deeds,
A List Of Virtues

JORDAN WAS A PRETTY INTERESTING GUY; most people who knew him thought that. He knew it himself, and considered himself, among other complimentary and diabolical attributes he possessed, nothing less than *interesting* in a wholly non-arrogant way. But those who knew him, in fact, didn't really know him very well at all. Jordan knew that, too.

He was a tough-to-slot guy and he both liked – no, *loved* - and abhorred that about himself. He was what you might call "polar opposites" though not in a schizophrenic way, but in more of a broad-scope, wide-ranging style, which occasionally encompassed seemingly incongruous but almost always fairly-balanced positions. He loved "fooling" people in a sweet but almost larcenous manner, yet he prized authenticity in people above everything else. See what I mean?

Jordan knew a lot of shit about a lot of shit. He was a kind of Zen "Jeopardy!" master, proudly filled with an impressive amount of generally useless knowledge – impressive to those who possessed less than him but useless, though, to pretty much everyone else. As much as he embraced this esoteric treasure chest of facts and figures, he also knew and quietly understood his fraudulence.

All this knowledge was good for small talk at parties, unleashed on attractive-yet unsuspecting women in bars (or at said parties) and with strangers who innocently engaged him on the train for whom he'd held the door open for them. He always made it a point to hold doors open for people, especially women, especially unattractive women because he knew it made their day since no one, pretty much ever, held doors open for them. But Jordan did. It was on his list of deeds and virtues.

The list, like Jordan, seemed to embody both sweetness and brutality: kind to the ugly and less fortunate; dismissive to the igno-rant and arrogant. Jordan's list was a Gemini dream and sometimes a Hulk-like nightmare, the duality occasionally tearing at his skin with rage and quiet glee, sadness, confusion and then delight. He made and re-made the list, editing, smiling, sneering, erasing and pleading to no-one and everyone, anyone at all, who would or could see the lines between the lines. They didn't need to read between the lines, just be able to "see" them and nod.

The list was long and exacting but necessary to create. It had that block-and-tackle aspect of the "good" Jordan, yet it stayed in symmetri-cal balance with the idea Jordan disdained so much, that of the "tightly controlled message" which usually meant something embarrassing was being hidden. So he left open a few more neatly numbered spaces at the end of the page for anyone who wanted to add to it.

It was a good list. A proper list, not the "half-a-job" he always frowned upon with others who invariably disappointed him. He was happy with its misery and mastery and felt it was an honest reflection of him. All of him, especially the unseen him. It was his list, and soon it would be someone else's list.

He folded it neatly into thirds, slipped it into the self-sealing envelope and slipped the envelope into the old English desk drawer.

It was then, and only then, that he put the gun in his mouth.

Lovers for Friends

Lunch

"AH COME ON, MAN, SHE WAS UGLY!" Martin half-smiled at Rocco across our lunch table when he mentioned Marie Carmen.

"Hey, ugly girls, just like ugly guys, need sex too!" Rocco correctly replied. He was also correct that ugly girls appreciated the attention even more than the pretty ones, who saw it more as validation of their (vain) sexiness.

"What about Alba? She was very nice!"

"She was - very cute and very sweet *and*, well, appeared to love *jamon* a bit too much, shall we say? Gracias pero no."

"Luz? She was *very* sexy – if you reject her I might make a try!" said Rocco.

"She *was* sexy – maybe *too* sexy for me but also not interested in me, that was coldly obvious. She was a bit too in love with herself and her stupid mobile phone for my taste."

"Remember Eva, the Basque?"

"Oh yes I do," Martin replied. "But she talked to your girlfriend basically all night and her lack of English made it boring for me, not cute."

"Look man", Martin said to Rocco, "you are the most James Bond guy I know. Think, brother, think!" Martin implored. "You must have a friend? A long-ago lover that just didn't work out? Maybe the woman who cuts your hair that you have always been very hot for and you wouldn't mind sharing with me but you don't want to mess up your professional relationship? Someone from your office or better yet, a close friend of whoever your girlfriend is this week (or month)?"

"You know my standards, which are perhaps a bit higher than yours!" Martin smirked. "I've given you wide latitude in your search: preferably petite, but not taller (or heavier!) than me, despite it being a mostly "horizontal relationship."

"Short blond hair, wavy brown hair, long curly black hair – *ni importa.*"

"Dark eyes and an attitude like a furious flamenco dancer or blonde, sweet and always-happy like a puppy that never gets older or has a bad day."

"Speaks multiple Mediterranean languages – that would be very nice. For sure, her English must be at least acceptable – we can work through the things she might not understand, and of course, vice versa."

"Una *musa* would be great, but probably impossible, not by your definition, but by mine."

"And I don't mind at all if she smoked. I might even prefer it. Solo digo..."

"Al fin, an agent provocateur! Sweet enough to be playful and push my buttons, but understands and replies *"Si Capitano... si mi Commandante..."* Martin laughed out loud, only half kidding.

"So, Sr. Bond, can you spin through your contacts list or shake your Tinder garbage can upside down? Stop being so *egoista* and keeping them all for yourself and find someone we can double date with?"

Laughing, Rocco said "Okay, okay, there are many, many girls out there, as you know, but the right one, for either me or you, well, it's not so easy. *Pero, mi amigo,* I will try. *Vale, quieres un cortado y postre?"*

Rocco and Martin had met many years before but had lost touch with the change of jobs that had originally brought them together. A "here's-my-new-contact-info" letter followed by a sudden Christmas card along with Martin's move to Barcelona reunited them. They were genuine friends and true fans of many of the same things: food and wine, the beach, basketball and *futbol*, Catalan culture and definitely, each in their own way, beautiful women.

Rocco was a rising executive at a high-end global jewelry design company, handsome by anyone's definition, very fit and lots of fun to be around.

Martin was a few years older than Rocco, semi-retired and living in Barcelona as a consultant for an international human rights organization helping refugees. He was warm, approachable, charming and alone.

Amuse Bouche

"GERMA, I THINK I FOUND SOMEONE" said the WhatsApp message from Rocco.

"Oh? *Detalls, detalls, si us plau*" replied Martin using the little Catalan that he knew.

"Hmmm no – you will just have trust my judgment. Do you?"

"Of course I do, in everything, you know that: *tot.*"

"Okay, we meet at "Restaurant Llamber" at 21.00."

Well, well, thought Martin, here we go! Actually, he looked forward to *any* night out with some company. Yes, indeed, Martin loved his solitude and nights sitting on the bench in Placa de Sant Agusti Vell having a cigar and watching the world of the *El Born* neighborhood stroll by, but still, he craved a night of fun, food, friends and all the possibilities of a date, by any definition. Refugee work was draining and lonely, though spiritually fulfilling.

"Yes!" Martin replied with enthusiasm, "but wait. Despite my trust in your judgement, we should have a sign between us, a signal for me to let you know you made a good choice. Or not."

"Maybe it will be immediate. Upon sight. Maybe it will be after the *tapa del casa*, the *amuse bouche*. Something subtle but definitive, something to confirm to each other, either an "ho-lahh" or "ho-nooo"."

"Maybe I just bump your foot under the table – one tap for yes, two taps for no."

"No, wait, *mejor*: I will turn my charm meter all the way up if I am intrigued and offer her *un brindis*, that I will personally and "graciously" propose a "nice to meet you" (while looking directly at her) and "nice to see you again" (to you and su chica del dia, Maribel) with a "*salut y pelas.*"

If there is no interest, then no *brindis*, just a "*salut.*" Good?

"Good! And I will not tell you more other than to say she is an old friend from Girona, though I *will* say she is 'the girl'. Nada mas."

Okay nos vemos a las nueve."

Pre-Game

THERE IS SO MUCH IN LIFE that is happenstance. Serendipity. The moment, the crystal moment when you meet someone for the first time, anyone at all. Judgments silently spin like a water spout with smiles real and fake flying across the space. Then the moment passes, but the perception, correct or incorrect, often hangs around longer than maybe it should, waiting for either affirmation or alteration.

In excited anticipation, Martin pressed Rocco for just a bit more information, a few basic details for a pencil sketch, but not enough for a full portrait to poison his imagination or expectations.

Being the good but devilish friend he was, Rocco offered this:

Okay, so the girl, I tell you, is THE GIRL. We dated once or twice a few years ago but just never clicked. She just turned fifty-three, mature attitude but physically young and in a great, very athletic shape. Really sensual with long brown hair, dark eyes like a gypsy. She got married very young and divorced after a few years. She very much likes her independence. She is intelligent, well educated, dresses the right way for every situation. She can confidently contribute to any kind of conversation and is also very funny with a smart and not silly or girlish humor, though her humor is sometimes a bit "under the table". She loves to eat great food and drink good wines. She is a fascinating girl and you won't want the meal to end because you feel so happy being with her. And for all of her "serious maturity" I have it on good authority that she is a tiger in bed. I tell you: the girl!

Well **THIS** I better get ready for! Martin thought. And so began a series of decisions:

Haircut, yes or no?

Beard trim, but not too close. It gets scratchy when clipped closely and *if* we get lucky, well, "beard burn" is not the thing I want her to remember after the first date.

Nails clipped. Eyebrows trimmed.

What to wear? Sports jacket? Hmm trying too hard.

Let me check the temperature for that night – black T-shirt? Sexy but too casual. Okay, definitely my lucky purple shirt.

Dark jeans. Shoes I only wear for dates (which were, um, barely worn)

Smell nice – find a cologne! - but don't overdo it, Spanish style.

Do I get there first? If so, do I wait outside? Hmm no, looks too anxious.

Do *they* get there first? Do they wait outside and watch me approach them, sizing me up along the way? Or do I wait for them to arrive first, sit at the table and then I make my "entrance". Hmm maybe…

And then, of course, what if I get lucky? What if every star in the Mediterranean sky shines on just the two of us? Well then: fresh towels in the bathroom; candles and music all ready to go; clean sheets on the bed; gin, tonic, red, white and cava, tequila and (for me!) Moscatel! Plus, make sure I have coffee, milk, y croissants…*just in case!*

As it is said, you never get a second chance to make a first impression. If this were a kind of "interview", then from Rocco's description, Martin wanted the job.

The Double Date

MARTIN WALKED SUPER SLOWLY DOWN to the restaurant, checking his watch as if a bomb were going to explode. Strolling while absentmindedly looking into windows at things he could not care less about, he did not want to overload on adrenaline and definitely did *not* want to get sweaty before arriving, like a racehorse foaming at the neck before the Kentucky Derby. Also, he wanted to be just a bit late, to let the anticipation build. But how late? Five minutes is not really late. Fifteen minutes? Fifteen minutes is officially late in the world of lateness, but in Spain, Martin found fifteen minutes to be perfectly on time. Okay then, twelve minutes late. Exactly twelve minutes: Martin just couldn't risk being *actually* late.

He had ached to but resisted asking Rocco for a photo of...of... hmm what *was* her name? He was so excited about the date he realized he had never asked. After they agreed about all the details of the place and time, Martin had decided to call her "Leticia from Galicia". But by the end of this night, she surely would be "Venus Aphrodite" because the only thing, the only words, the only sensations that came to his mind and body were "VA VA VA VOOM!" when he saw her.

La Cena

HE TOOK A DEEP BREATH and thought about which to enter as, happy funny Martin or mysterious, thoughtful, sly *"c'est si bon"* Martin. He decided to appeal to her desire for fun first and went with happy and funny, to first gauge her reaction. And lighten the mood.

He saw them as soon as he entered the doors, straight ahead toward the back. The wine was already on the table, a good sign – Rocco loved good, serious wine. Rocco sat facing the door with "Leticia" on his left and Maribel across from him, thereby allowing Martin to sit directly across from Leticia as well as giving her a full view of his entrance. Martin sucked his stomach in and made his way to the table.

Rocco caught Martin's eye: big smile, arms up and a gentle mambo-shoulder shimmy shake. Martin looked directly at Rocco and *then* Leticia as he entered, making *sure* they locked eyes and confirming her smile. She might not have immediately known it was him, but she definitely *hoped* it was as he bumped into the waitress and apologized in pantomime making all three of them laugh and having her think "Hmmm who is *this* funny guy? Oh, it's "him" as Martin's arrival at the table coincided with Rocco laughingly announcing "there he is". He bowed deeply to them with three smiles shining back at him.

A hug for Rocco, two kisses for Maribel and then, crossing over behind Maribel, he turned his charm-meter up to eleven and took Leticia's hand as if to shake it. But then, looking her straight in her lovely eyes, with a look on her face of "Oh how lovely, he is going to kiss my hand!" he raised it to *his* lips and kissed his own hand! Everyone laughed when he said "Hey I am a gentleman!" but you could immediately tell Leticia bought it, and thought Martin was very cute. Successful entrance! Post position established! Intrigue at full throttle!

She was, at first glance, someone to be taken seriously and *all* that Rocco had described: a grown woman, not a "girl" with just a tiny but definitive wrinkle around her eyes. Mature and confident with a natural and easy smile paired with just a hint of a hidden reserved-judgment look in her eye. Fair enough, thought Martin, I'm gonna blowtorch that coolness into a puddle. That secret *"brindis"* he and Rocco had agreed upon did not take very long to take shape with his warm, direct and soulful toast. Rocco and Martin slyly winked at each other.

"Rocco? Always a pleasure. Maribel, so nice to see you again!" *Cin cin* – "And Leticia, I am honoured to be at this table with you" he warmly and rather dramatically intoned along with a devastatingly charming and wry accompanying smile. He knew she got the message, and she, he sensed, returned it, with a sparkling smile and warm *"Gracias Martin, igualmente"* nod of her head and shake of her long hair. They *were* definitely and immediately interested in each other. *Ho-laaaa* indeed!

In reality, she *was* perfect in so many ways: silk blouse, matching pearl-and-gold necklace and bracelets highlighting her elegant hands with a beautiful frosted polish on her nails. Tight jeans that framed her athletic shape beautifully. Simple, almost imperceptible makeup and gypsy-hoop earrings. But you can be sure, as she had stayed seated when he entered, that Martin, oops, "casually" dropped his napkin about fifteen minutes into the meal, just to check her shoes – sorry/not sorry to be shallow, he thought, but I judge women by their shoes! Was she dressed for seduction? Sensibility? What signal would she send? All the answers rested in her *"tacones"*. And every reply was "I'm-ready-to-take-a-chance-on-something-tonight-why-not?" with her colorful 10 cm daggers. So, the outside *was* sensational. Now for the inside.

Martin never felt the need to "entertain" Leticia during the dinner, though she did react positively and honestly to the comments, observations, charm and sweet sexiness he threw at the table in the course of it all. Better still, she did not agree with everything he said and Martin admired that very much. He returned her glances, as well as her penetrating stares as they both tried to peek beneath their attractive surfaces, their mind's-eye spinning from holding hands and walking on the beach to raw, hot, clothes-ripping, buttons-flying barely one meter inside the door (any door!) romantic chaos. He also listened to her closely and found she was, indeed, smart, thoughtful and more than skin-deep in both her intellect and charm. *Fuck!* She was really something, on 100 levels.

She also had a sweet little "tell" as poker players and psychologists call it, a small affectation of the hands and mind. She "absent-mindedly" spun a small ring on the right hand of her pinky in the design of an infinity symbol during the conversation, especially, Martin noticed, when she listened as he spoke to the topic at hand. It was an act of attention, of entrancement.

The dinner was genuinely delicious with inventive, creative food. It was also satisfyingly long: unlike restaurants in New York, here you really could *enjoy* a meal and you "owned" the table until *you* were ready to leave, not when the restaurant wanted you out. The conversation was like jazz: free flowing, clever, opinionated solos with un-syncopated off-ramps and tendrils detouring things with excited explanations. But underpinning it all was a warm and steady rhythmic beat like an undertow that always brought the conversation and the conversationalists back to the table. They talked politics, sports, Catalan independence, the cost of American life, real estate, movies and all manner of topics. It was, in a word, delightful. Of course, Martin the Pessimist thought something had to go "wrong" now, no?

"It's Getting Late – Is It Getting Late for You?"

THE COFFEE CAME – THREE *café cortado* and one *café ristretto* (Rocco). Leticia carefully but discreetly watched Martin "address" his coffee. He rejected the offering of sugar, which silently pleased her very much, a bit of the cherry on the evening. On the flip side, Martin sensed he was being "watched" as he had been all night long, and he acted accordingly – stylishly slipping his index finger into a tucked corner of the napkin and wiping the corner of his moustache with a bit of flourish after each bite; being careful not to fiddle foolishly with table accoutrements; mindful not to use his hands in a too-dramatic manner in case he knocked over her glass of wine.. Now that the coffee had arrived, knowing he was being observed he delicately slipped and slid the back of his spoon slowly around the rim of the cup after a few perfunctory swizzles, like a pizza maker circling the sauce on the dough, leaving a delicious stain and eliciting a quietly arched eyebrow from Leticia, who tried to hide behind the last sips of the delicious Flor de Pingus . That coffee move suggested a seductive caress and neither missed the symbolism. The group unfolded from the table after more than three fantastic hours and the men helped slip the coats of the ladies over their shoulders.

Not wanting to overplay his hand, Martin left the next steps open to the others to decide. He did not want to push but he did not want to stand there being an indecisive man who did not have an opinion. So he offered a few scenarios and agreed to agree with whatever the group said to do next.

He knew there would be time again with Leticia – they talked about places to visit for a nice day trip together outside the city, deep in Catalunya, as well as the possibility of a long weekend in Marseille where Leticia was going for a realtor's convention in April.

So at this critical moment, after Martin graciously offered to invite everyone for the dinner and good-naturedly "fought" for the check with Rocco, they faced a decision, with many options but only one outcome:

Option #1 – Rocco y Maribel walk to the car in the parking lot to drive back to Girona while Martin and Leticia wait together for them to return, confirm their mutual intrigue, kiss gently, then quickly and definitively agree to connect very soon. Leticia whispers "I'd love to stay, Martin, but I have to go home and take care of my dogs". On the way to their respective homes, both Martin and Leticia send sweet "so nice to meet you" SMS messages within one minute of saying goodbye. Lots of heart and kisses emoji's.

Option #2 – Hugs and kisses and smiles and sweet goodbyes at the car. Then Leticia tries to strangle Rocco from the backseat for such a horrible evening, cries all the way back to Girona and never contacts Martin again. Martin briefly considers suicide when he hears of this, but then thinks "Fuck it, *que sera sera*." Rocco and Martin remain good friends.

Option #3 – They decide the night is still young and agree to go to a Brazilian tequila bar nearby for more drinks and laughs. Even a little tequila is too much for Martin – embarrassing mayhem ensues.

Option #4 - They decide the night is still young and agree with the ladies idea to go to Luz de Gas for dancing. Neither Rocco nor Martin are enthusiastic about this option, but go along with the idea.

Then, after the club, any one of the following sub-outcomes might occur:

Outcome #1 (a) – Rocco, Maribel and Leticia go back to the hotel they secured, expecting a late night with lots of alcohol. Martin goes home. They all have breakfast together the next morning.

Outcome #1 (b) – Rocco and Maribel go back to the hotel they secured, expecting a late night with lots of alcohol. Martin and Leticia go back to his apartment for drinks and music. Sweet sanity prevails and they all have breakfast together the next morning.

Outcome #1 (c) – They all go back to Martin's two-bedroom/ two bathroom apartment for drinks and music. They all fall asleep, drunk, with their clothes on. They all have breakfast together the next morning.

Although Rocco had had a coffee he was, in fact, pretty tired, it being the end of another busy week. He was always an excellent driver and he'd made the trip from Girona along the AP 7 into Barcelona so often he could make the drive while reading and shaving. But Maribel could see he was yawning so she offered to drive – she only had one glass of wine, as she preferred white but did not want to upset the vibe of the red-wine loving table. So after warm hugs and a final group laugh, Maribel slid behind the wheel, Leticia by her side and Rocco sprawled out in the backseat.

It's about an hour's drive to Girona. By the time they reached Montcada, Rocco was fast asleep. Leticia was still buzzing from the dinner and meeting Martin, (now called "Mar-teen") chatting with Maribel and playing with the radio with her left hand while stretching her right hand out the open window, gliding in the wind and thinkingsmilingdreaming happily of the evening.

The AP-7 runs along the Costa Brava to the Languedoc region of France. The Clasquin 18-wheel truck was loaded with oranges from Morocco, textiles from Egypt and auto parts from three Renault factories in France. For truck drivers all around the world, nighttime travel is the quickest way to cover the distance between two points and Gerard "Bebe" Lafitte had been running this route for years. The guys at the Clasquin depot called him "Bebe" because he was a BIG guy, almost 300 pounds.

Martin, smiling deeply, sunk into the backseat of a taxi, chin in hand, staring out the window. His mind was spinning with a thousand images, half with the brilliant evening he had just spent, and half with the imagined events to come with Leticia. Their goodnight kiss would surely keep him up until sunrise as he licked his lips over and over to savor its taste. Like the wine, her kiss tasted full of lust and deliciousness, promise and desire.

When Martin got home, he opened the floor-to-ceiling windows and turned on some sexy music, setting the volume down to two.

He slipped out onto his terrace and lit a small cigar to dream big dreams, to let the smoke rise as whispers of thanks toward heaven for an incredible night.

Bebe ate too much and drank too much. He knew that and his wife often reminded him of it, though for the most part, good naturedly, whenever she tried to wake him from the couch to go to bed with him fast asleep after another big meal.

Maribel drove quietly and listened to Leticia's excited but restrained thoughts and ideas about the evening. Maribel really liked Rocco and while she only casually knew Leticia through Rocco, she enjoyed being with her and meeting Martin. It was a fun "double-date".

It only took a few seconds for Bebe's truck to cross the centerline. He had been nodding off and snapping back to attention for almost half the trip post-dinner from Montpellier. He used to boast how he could drive the route in his sleep.

He couldn't.

Maribel was killed instantly. Leticia was thrown from the car through the open window and died moments before the ambulance arrived. Rocco survived, having been belted into the back seat, though five ribs were crushed and one lung collapsed from the impact against the life-saving seatbelt.

Martin showered the cigar smoke from himself and finally fell asleep about three a.m., but not before he sent a text to Leticia, a whispered kiss, and a thank you for a sweet and magical night.

"Gracias por todo, Leticia. Por usted. Hasta muy pronto!" The message with a few bouncing heart emoji's buzzed and glowed from her cracked mobile phone screen. The police found it lying in the weeds of a ditch off the side of the road, near where they found Leticia. It was just beyond the reach of her right hand, where her silver infinity ring was shining in the lights of the ambulance.

Now batting, #33 - Jesus Christ

OK, I'M AS RELIGIOUS AS THE NEXT GUY. No, probably more so. A true believer, though with more than a dash of present-day realism sprinkled on my communion host.

But am I the only person who questions the religious comportment of athletes, particularly baseball players, who cross themselves two and three times before stepping into the batter's box? I mean, are they really whispering "In the name of the father, most holy precious blood and the fruit of thy womb Jesus, help me knock one up the alley to the opposite field against this rookie"? Aren't there *other* things God would like you to ask him for? Like an on-time departure from Kennedy Airport? The last shirt in *that* shade of blue? In a large, please. The exacta, just once? World peace and global un-warming? A fat admissions envelope from your child's first choice of college. A taxi, in the rain, no matter where, with just the snap of my God-given fingers? Aren't these more worthy paeans to God than an RBI on a Thursday afternoon in St. Louis?

Old Married Couple

"WHAT DO YOU WANT TO DO TONIGHT?"

"I don't care. What do you want to do?"

"That's not an answer. The answer to a question with a question is not an answer."

"But darling," he said dryly, "I'm easy. I'm happy to do pretty much what you want to do."

"Steven, I think all day and make decisions all week. Don't make me do it on a Saturday too."

"But how wonderful is your life that you can choose the path it takes, with little-to-no resistance from me?"

"It's not wonderful: your ambivalence is exhausting!"

"It's not ambivalence: its compromise."

"You know, you're an ass. Don't you have a single opinion on what to do, what *you* want to do?"

"I do, but I am also eternally open to suggestion, and presumably we can find common ground, perhaps even happily so, *darling*" he said through gritted teeth.

"Okay". She paused to take her boiling emotions off the fire. "How about a movie?"

"Sure. What do you want to see?"

"Well, you generally don't like the movies I like."

"Not true, we have sat through thousands of movies in our life together."

"Well, how about X?"

"No, not that. I mean, if I retain a drop of opinion, I would vote no on that one. But there surely are others, no?"

"Okay then, what do *you* want to see?"

"Hmmm, let me look. – Okay how about Y?"

"Where is it playing and at what time?" she said unenthusiastically, hoping for a way out.

"Cineplex at 7:30 or 10 p.m."

"I hate that theater, you know that. And *if* we go, we have to leave in 10 minutes, or you'll fall asleep at the 10 o'clock show, sooooo…."

"Okayyyyyyyyyy how about Movie A? "

"*You* want to see *that*?"

"I would…if you wanted to."

"But it's not your first choice."

"No, but why does it have to be *my* first choice? My first choice will leave both of us unhappy, because you'll hate my first choice and hate having to do what only I wanted to do, even though you are begging for my first choice"

(The refrain "a happy wife is a happy life" begins to sing-song through his head.)

"What time is it playing?"

"8:20 or 10:40."

"I don't think you're gonna like it."

"It didn't sound bad, and given the options…."

"See if there's anything on Netflix?"

"No, let's go out. There, how's that for an opinion?"

"Why, don't you have dinner planned and cooked already?"

"Ohhhhhh here we go….."

"Speaking of dinner, what do you want to eat?"

"I don't care, what do you feel like?"

Blood on the Roses

Ralph

"When you come out of the storm, you won't be the same person who walked in. That's what this storm's all about."

HARUKI MURAKAMI

UNLIKE MOST PEOPLE PRETTY MUCH around the world, Ralph Neumann looked forward to Monday mornings and getting back to work, because weekends for Ralph amounted to yard work, bad movies and bad food ordered from takeout menus. Add in errands, laundry, chips and porn and the reality for Ralph was, his job was the escape from his life, not the other way around.

This particular Monday, however, was going to be very, very different. Ralph had barely sat down at his desk with a bacon-egg-and-cheese-on-a-roll and a "regulah" coffee when Tina poked her head over the partition and told him Michael ("never 'Mike'") wanted to see him in his office. Ralph blanched and then gulped, his mind racing, thinking what he could possibly have done wrong? It was only Monday! Michael did not chit-chat with Ralph even when things were going right – his mocking "Ralphie boooyy!" was always said in soft derision, not camaraderie, so this could not be good.

In fact, it was great.

He grabbed a bunch of current manifests to soak up the blood in case he was about to be slaughtered for something he could not imagine and did a very quick check of the "scoreboard" in the middle of the operations center, a giant video screen showing a real-time satellite feed of all the company's "CIR" (cargo-in-route).

"Hey Ralphie boooyy, sit down. How was your weekend?" Uh oh, Ralph thought, knowing that his face was flushed red with anticipatory doom: the deadly, empty pleasantries before the execution. This *cannot* be good!

Omitting the parts about the Costco-sized bag of chips and the hours-worth of porn, he stammered "Um, pretty good. Did some yard work mostly. How about you?"

"Ah not much different than you-yard work, washed the cars- but with my wife yelling at me most of the time!" Forced chuckles ensued.

Well, enough useless small talk, they both thought. "Anyway, I want you to know that I recognize you work hard, and you work hard at being careful and thorough. So I'd like to send you to the Posidonia Conference this year, both to learn and as a kind of reward for your effort. You good with that?"

How can one be slack-jawed yet sputtering? Ralph was both – as well as *immensely* relieved.

"Oh! Uummm, yeah, wow that would be *great*! Thank you so much. I hear the guys talking about it every year. Um, so, how do I do this? Who do I talk to"? he replied, elated, confused but, as per Ralph, low key about it.

"Just talk to Tina and she will set it all up for you. And keep up the good work. I definitely want to hear *your* crazy stories afterwards. The Greek crews always cause good trouble and the Filipinos drink like no one I've ever seen!"

"Well, okay!" Ralph allowed himself a laugh, an excited, ooh-ba-by-I'm-one-of-the-guys-now kind of laugh. "Thank you very much Michael!"

"Just remember," Michael admonished with a dirty grin "what happens on the road, stays on the road. Once the captain turns off the seatbelt sign, you will be over open, unrestricted waters and beyond the international fishing limit of 12 nautical miles. Which means: start the party! So definitely have fun. Just be careful!

"Oh, and I actually expect a full report on the conference when you return."

Ralph liked his job enough, and had risen ever so slowly at "League Leader Cargo", an international cargo shipping brokerage firm. Working for LLC, LLC. made him quietly laugh, since he had never been the leader in anything in his life: not in sports, not with girls, not in school, not the model of his car or TV or the clothes he wore. He was never in the lead, not even when shooting water into the clown's mouth at a carnival. Ralph was always a "back of the pack" kinda guy, and he came to understand and accept this, consciously sitting in the back of a movie theater, a lecture hall, or an airplane. There was comfort to be taken by being in the shadows, and not at the bow of the ship for anything–less to hit or be hit by head on.

It's been said that the view from the back is of everyone else's ass, but he saw how others in the company would get blasted when their projections were wrong and their show-off estimates proved to be *very* expensive for the organization. You didn't make too many of those mistakes at LLC, LLC. before *you* were shipped out. While there were bonuses to be had for on-time or early arrivals, Ralph was happy knowing he could live within his means without the risk. The spotlight did not suit him, literally or figuratively, due to the shine on his prematurely bald head. One terribly expensive mistake three years ago terrified him, and he'd never felt so fat or stupid like that before. He vowed he would stay in his lane and never shoot for the stars again: he just wasn't very good at it, despite his daredevil dreams.

Ralph was the kind of guy who carried his wallet in the *front* pocket of his always-baggy pants.

A mellow and easy-going man, he didn't want any trouble from anyone, anywhere, at any time. He barely even honked his car horn for fear of a road rage incident. Sure, a real temper existed, but he tamped that temper way down inside. Ralph never really "…came from behind for the win…", but he tried to at least cut the distance and make a respectful showing in whatever he did, from bowling at a company outing right down to the rare dates with women.

Oh, dates with women! How Ralph struggled, and struggled with his desire *not* to struggle, but to be calm, casual, glib, and carefree. In command. The captain of **his** ship. He stumbled through Bumble and Tinder was a damp disappointment. Ralph spent hours and hours swiping and hoping and frowning and deleting and clumsily steering off course of so many dating sites that he had actually made a New Year's resolution a few years back to boycott all of them.

But like the drug love and loneliness is, a howler monkey on his back, he returned, eventually and often.

Glasses or contacts? New shirt, false backdrops, high bravado or humble and sweet, Ralph just could not find the right formula to break through and connect with someone, mostly online but even in real life. Yes, he did manage to arrange a few coffee chats over the years, but those who agreed to meet him were themselves so hideous, Ralph thought, that even *he* could do better next time. So he forged ahead, undaunted but undated.

Ralph gathered himself back at his desk for a minute. He first gave Oscar, his cubicle mate, the thumbs up and then slipped off to the men's room. He began to slowly wash his hands as Nelson from the Maritime Charter Division finished washing his. After Nelson *finally* left, he peeked along the ground to make a quick stall-check to see if anyone else was in there. Free and clear, Ralph stood in front of the mirror and jumped for joy! He silently screamed with unbridled happiness, pumped his fist like Tiger Woods and twirled himself like Cristiano Ronaldo after a goal. He was going to Posidonia! In Barcelona, no less!

Back at his desk, red-faced but ecstatic, he quickly replied to an urgent customer email: "Yes Marco, A/G/W, W/P, Prince of Algiers should be in Durban by 24 June, W/O/G but we feel confident."

And then he went on the Posidonia website and let himself dream. Maybe, just maybe, this was his chance, to leave old "Ralphie boooyy" at JFK for the "new" Ralph Neumann! To unstick himself from who he was and had always been and bring forth the mythical and heretofore unknown-to-the-world "Super Neumann!" Besides, no one else from LLC, LLC would be there and he wouldn't know anyone else at the conference, so he could be whoever he wanted to be

And maybe, just maybe, he would get laid.

Ralph was feeling silently giddy that night and it was everything to contain his happiness. Ralph was not often happy, by anyone's definition. Not morose, not depressed, a bit withdrawn, semi-shy, but definitely not *happy*. He kept a barely-smiling equilibrium about him, mostly because there wasn't all that much about Ralph's life that gave him happiness, much less real joy.

Being "alone" caused Ralph to bottle up emotions most people share, though these days, everyone wants to share everything, whether you want to be the share-ee or not. At work, on TV, behind the wheel of their honking car, the way people loudly announced themselves in the aisles of the mall with their look-at-me swagger, big fat asses and ridiculous outfits; on the beach in bathing suits that should have never left the dressing room and, holy cannoli, on the internet. Sharing just wasn't Ralphs thing, that's all, though at work, it *did* make him feel nice to have someone share with him their new baby picture, or invite him to the conference room for (always someone else's) surprise birthday party. He had even gotten used to the mocking "Ralphie boooyy" when he entered a conference or breakroom. Generally though, he never bothered anyone and kept his mouth shut, two qualities highly prized in an office. But no one ever invited him to lunch either, or let him know there were donuts in the kitchen until all that was left were crumbs and an empty box. He knew he didn't *need* the donut, but not being told or included directly, hurt. Ralph was an office afterthought. A pity invite. A part of him liked it that way but to be sure, a part of him sighed deeply, mostly in the car on the way home, at the lack of a "hug" and someone to share something with, even if he had nothing really to share.

At least Oscar, his cubicle mate, was a decent guy who never joined in the mocking games. Oscar was a single soul himself, and understood Ralph's unease. They would share their dating sorrows and frustrations, but cut them short when it got a bit too personal. They even tried, once, to hang out on a weekend but realized it was too awkward to be actual friends and went back to being good office colleagues. Oscar was also the only person Ralph thought he was "superior" to, on a social scale, which did not say much about Oscar, at least to Ralph. Still, Oscar was a decent guy and they enjoyed each other as work friends, sharing opinions, laughs, take-out lunches and office gossip with a like-minded (sad) soul.

When Ralph was growing up, he knew all the kids in the neighborhood but couldn't honestly say he was actual friends with any. He was always the last guy picked for any game. Big, slow-those damn chips!-and bulky, he was always the "c'mon-we-need-one-more-guy-to-play" fill-in.

He did, though, *once*, have his moment of neighborhood glory and (fleeting) legend: he sometimes served as the goalie when the kids played street hockey, being the biggest obstacle in front of the net. One afternoon, two of the guys, Alex Hubbleton and Peter Garcia, announced that they had gotten a challenge to play the "Lewis Avenue Boys" in the park behind St. Sebastian's Prep.

Given Ralphs bulk, they decided to use him as a kind of enforcer, despite his slowness, and park him in front of the net as a defensive deterrent rather than as the goalie. The Lewis Avenue Boys were an arrogant bunch of assholes who went to a different school, but the sisters of two of their guys knew Alex and Peter from their church Sunday school and the challenge was made.

The game was close and the Lewis Avenue Boys were surprised and getting frustrated at how much better Ralphs team turned out to be. Consequently, things got a bit chippy by the end of the "ten-goals-win" and some fool, who took Ralph to also be a fool, decided to get rough in the goal crease with him, chopping at his shin guards and finally, giving him a hard cross-check right across his shoulder blades. *Big* mistake! Hulk-like, that shot with the stick in his back **hurt** and flipped a switch in him. Ralph spun around, looked the player dead in his eye, and after many years of watching the New York Rangers drop-the-gloves-and-go-at-it on TV, in one smooth muscle-memory motion (despite *never* having done so before) Ralph dropped his stick and gloves, grabbed the players shirt chest high, and clocked him in the head! The beast was out of the cage!

He then, further imitating the pro's, reached behind the guy on his staggering way down to his knees and yanked his jersey over his head, immobilizing his arms and putting the poor sucker in perfect position to take another thundering shot to the side of his head.

Shocking even for himself, Ralph was snorting and ready for more! The guys on his team whooped and paired off while the Lewis Avenue Boys tucked in their tails in and called "game over". If Ralph could have been lifted on their shoulders, he would have been, but the guys celebrated and hollered all the way back to their neighborhood with "One-Punch Neumann"! He was a hero!

For all of 48 hours.

The story made its way around gym class on Monday, getting Ralph a few pats on the back and more than a few odd but "fearful" glances from guys he never knew.

And that was that. No party invites, no lets-hang-out call ups. Just back to being plain old Ralph, the slow, fat goalie in the street games.

For Ralph, though, it was pure magic and a side of him emerged that he never even dreamed of before. "LADIES AND GENTLE-MEN, IN THE RED CORNERRRRRR, PLEASE WELCOME 'ONE PUNCH NEUMANN'!!" he mouthed into his bedroom mirror as he did a boxers warm-up dance! The Hulk indeed! A few less bags of chips and a few more dollars spent on Hulk comic book followed and for a *long* time, Ralph (quietly) exulted in his unknown powers. But that guy really cracked him across his back, and Ralph knew it was not a hockey play, but a shove-this-fat-guy-around play. He got what he deserved, Ralph thought. And so did Ralph as a result, at least for a little while.

A good and lonely son, Ralph was neglected by his father and doted on by his mother, who always seemed on the verge of madness if he was out of her sight (but never her mind) for too long. As luck (if one could call it that) would have it, the house right next door became available after Mrs. Tremonti passed away. Ralphs mother not-so-quietly pressed him to buy it directly from the family, whose three siblings now lived in Colorado, California and Maine and wanted nothing to do with it. It *did* kind of thrill him to finally be "inside" Maria Tremonti's room, after all those years of staring across the driveway and imagining what *that* would be like.

So he took it on as a project to get off the couch and more importantly, out of the house (even if it *was* only next door) and out from his mother's constant line-of-oversight, spending "his" inheritance from when his father died suddenly and far away. It was never really *his* inheritance, not as long as his mother was alive, but she doled out what was needed, as selfish as could be, to purchase the Tremonti place.

Ralph never enjoyed a penny of that money. He never splurged in any way; he never went to Las Vegas for a crazy weekend with the guys (there were no guys to go with, actually) or buy a ridiculous new car or even treat himself and his mother to a steak dinner. As it was locked in a bank account that required two signatures for every transaction, it might as well have been pinned inside his mother's oversized bra, that's how inaccessible it was. Given his "smotherly-love" upbringing, his mother might have loved for him to snuggle to her breast again for a couple of bucks.

To be sure, the Tremonti house did give Ralph more than a measure of freedom. It was freshly painted – simple off-white tones, said his mother – with new simple carpets and drapes she had picked out for Ralph "just to get you started." Mrs. Neumann lacked any sense of discernable "style" so there was nothing offensive, unique or personal about her tastes. It covered the spaces blandly and benignly.

Just like Ralph.

But it *was* his own place, all four walls and the roof. Okay, his mother, naturally, had a set of keys, but, newly emboldened, there was an agreement that she would not simply barge in at any moment she chose to. The house gave Ralph a true sense of both ownership and independence, no matter the provenance of the money. It was his and he (surprisingly even for him) firmly but gently drew a line for his mother: she was not to cross the yard and enter without permission. For the first time in a long time, he felt happy. Free, in measures great and small, to eat what he wanted, when he wanted to. To wash his own clothes without feeling like a little boy. To watch *any* TV program he chose to, at any hour of the night, as loud as he wanted.

And, as the saying goes, to dance like no one was watching. Finally, no one *might* be watching or listening and though no one could have guessed, Ralph loved to dance, albeit in front of the TV.

But there was no time for chips and porn now: he had to get ready for the big trip! New clothes! New shoes! Exchange dollars for Euros! Maybe a nice new pen and wristwatch for the conference lectures and surely social gatherings afterward! He quickly went to the Roosevelt Field Shopping Mall website and began to make a plan.

Ralph was a Merrell's/cargo pants/fleece-top-with-the-sleeves-always-too-long weekend kind of guy – his office attire was equally unremarkable and with the prospect of "Super Neumann" emerging at Posidonia, he knew it was time for a major upgrade. He would talk with Oscar about what to expect there and he would definitely talk with Tina tomorrow about the travel and conference details. Tonight he would do some research on the things to see and do in Barcelona.

Hmm, yes: Tina. She was always nice to him, always said good morning and let him know when Michael was in no mood for bad news. Maybe Tina could go with him to the mall and offer her feminine fashion point of view? Yes, yes! Tina was nice, he was sure she. . .might. Ralph wanted to look good, for once in his life.

Because maybe, no DEFINITELY, Ralph was going to get laid! Okay, the plan was ready: Shopping list! Barcelona sightseeing!

But first: a fresh bag of Ruffles (party size) and quick spin on Porn Hub.

Preflight Checklist

RALPH'S MIND SPUN LIKE A CENTRIFUGE with ideas, fears, excitement, images, possibilities and hopes, hopes that this really could be the moment he had long waited for: to break out of the same-old, same-old Ralph. Predictability had its place in life, until it metastasized into paralysis and Ralph knew he was on the fast track to that. He just never knew the road to take to get him out of his rut. Ralph sensed this was finally his chance to leave so much of his life behind, if only for one week, and both explore a new world, literally, and create a new world, figuratively, for himself.

Mrs. Neumann was initially happy with the news, and shared Ralph's sense of excitement and feeling of advancement in the office, and in himself.

For about a minute.

Then all those nervous smiles descended into just pure nerves, and worry and caution: Ralph would have none of it from her.

"Be careful Ralphie!"

"Don't worry Ma"

"Put a quarter in your shoe just in case!"

"Ma please, where was the last phone booth you saw?"

"I'll give you a small bottle of Clorox – make sure you wash all the fruit and vegetables before you eat them. And don't drink the water!"

"*MA*! It's 2023 for God's sake!"

"Don't call me during prime time – your Aunt Esther told me international calls are *crazy* expensive!"

"Don't worry – I'll txt you – yes every day, twice a day, I promise"

"Give me all the details – your flight numbers, your hotel, everything. Are you sure your phone will work over there? Is it on, like, the same frequency as ours?" How about your electric razor? You don't want to go looking like a bum to the conference!"

"Take some Pepto-Bismol with you! Do you have any or should we go to CVS and get some? Check what else you will need. Don't forget anything – you have no idea what kinds of things they sell over there!"

"*MAAAAA*! Stop already!" Ralph wailed, then leaned in for a hug and a kiss.

Every day, Ralph was feeling more and more like "the man" in the office. Word had gotten around that he was going to Posidonia and guys who had *never* spoken to him before - Terence the finance guy! Kosta, the Greek god that every woman died for! Even arrogant Joey Calabrese gave him a wink and a thumbs-up (though he then probably gave Ralph the finger afterwards) - stopped by his desk to say "Congrat's, have fun!" and the mandatory "watch out for the Filipinos and Greeks!" Damn, Ralph thought, what is *with* them?

Oscar also gave Ralph a bit of the lowdown – the conferences were, unsurprisingly, mostly boring but occasionally very interesting. They were really only good to scope out the women you planned to try and meet during the lunch break or the after-conference cocktail mixers. He did say to definitely go to the review of maritime law, which was always informative. The new product booths were fascinating for their diversity of all things oceanic; the after-hours cocktail parties were fun and stylish and if you get in with a group of – really, again?! – Greeks or Filipinos, prepare for a long, crazy night!

Oscar persuaded Tina to go with Ralph to Roosevelt Field for a shopping trip to upgrade himself for the conference. Ralph was crazy nuts! Meeting Tina Lopez-Castillo at Roosevelt Field on a Saturday! Shopping for Posidonia! Life had suddenly become fun!

Three new pairs of Bonobo's slacks. Some "UNTUCKit" shirts. New Loafers from Cole Haan. A nice-looking (and on-sale!) silver Nixon wristwatch. Two new sweaters to go with the shirts and pants. For the first time in forever he felt like one of the guys in the office, and maybe even like a "real man" outside of the office. Tina's presence and choices gave him a sense of confidence in his "new" look that he never had before. He reminded himself in the parking lot right before they met in front of the Cinnabon that he would *not* automatically say "um, no that's not really my style" to pretty much anything she suggested. He was on the precipice of "Super Neumann" and nothing, especially himself, was going to hold him back!

Departure

RALPH CHECKED AND RE-CHECKED HIS TICKET about three times per day, reading it over and over. He went online to see his seat and make sure it was still there – whoa, business class! He looked at travel guides, checked Rick Steves' recommendations, and then mostly ignored them – he was *not* going to wash his socks in the sink and wear the same pair of khaki's for a week! It's time for "Super Neumann!" he quietly declared over and over to himself.

On Thursday afternoon, he presented Tina with a small bouquet of flowers and his deep thanks for her kindness, for going shopping with him, preparing the details of his trip and basically being really, really kind to him. They both blushed, which made Ralph quite happy. Even though the flight was still twenty-four hours away, Ralph could barely contain himself. Oscar noticed his non-stop smile and had to laugh – they both did and Oscar gave Ralph a mini, awkward bro hug Thursday night.

"Have fun man! But not too much, okay? I want to know *every-thing* that goes on with you!"

"Okay, okay don't I tell you everything now?"

"Yeah, well there's not much to tell, is there?"

"You bastard" as they both laughed.

Ralph had not laughed with such giddiness in, maybe, forever. He poked his head in on Michael to say thank you again, asked if he could bring him anything back, and then thanked him again.

"Ralphie boooyy, don't forget, I want a report about the conference afterwards. And one more thing…

"Ha! I know Michael, I know!"

Along with his shopping spree with Tina, Ralph made sure he had the right electrical converter plugs packed away, new cologne (thank you Tina!), all fresh and new bathroom accessories, new socks (without holes), new underwear (also without holes) and T-shirts. He had gotten a haircut a week before, to buff off that "new haircut" dork-iness and had even downloaded the Duolingo app, which he'd been substituting (mostly) for porn at night.

He tried to relax Friday morning, though he was too keyed up to actually sleep "late." He checked and re-checked his passport, the hotel website, the conference website, the weather in New York and Barcelona, anything and everything to make sure he did not forget something and slap his forehead like old dumb Ralphie boooyy.

Given the ever-present traffic from Long Island, Tina had set up the Uber to collect him at 4:30 p.m. She said it would give him plenty of time to wander duty free and, more importantly, with his business-class ticket, relax and enjoy the private Delta Airlines lounge.

Hugs and kisses and a sniffle or three ensued during the text promises with Mrs. Neumann. Then, obsessively looking (and admiring!) his cheap but fancy new watch, he retreated to his house, made sure pretty much everything besides the refrigerator was unplugged, gathered his bags and watched out the window for the Uber while Mrs. Tremonti watched out the window for Ralph.

Feeling like a bigshot, he calmly greeted his Uber driver Sayd, climbed into the big boy back seat, took a deep breath, waved goodbye to his mother, who was clearly holding a handkerchief to her nose, and off they went. Sayd casually began a conversation about the destination, but Ralph was too deep in thought to talk much. Bigshot business men don't really talk to their Uber drivers, do they, he thought, so he wouldn't either. He wanted to "...act like he'd been there before..."and hoped Sayd had not seen his mother crying in the living room window. Now, he was wholly focused on the trip, and on himself, and the emergence of someone he had only dreamt of: a warm, confident, engaging, articulate shipping executive. To be and be seen as captain of his own ship and in full command of himself. Some swagger and arrogance, or at least a touch of both (hey baby steps, man, he thought to himself.) But he also thought "Let's do this Ralph! Let's fucking do this!" He adjusted Super Neumann's cape a bit in his head and breathed deeply.

"League Leader Cargo" treated their people well and the generous plan for Ralph's trip was a Friday night flight/Saturday morning arrival. He would have Saturday and Sunday to relax, get acclimated and sightsee a bit. The conference ran from Monday to Wednesday and then he had the luxury of exploring some more on Thursday with a Friday afternoon flight home.

Ralph calmly and confidently checked in at the desk. He felt slightly embarrassed by the lack of international stamps in his passport besides Aruba and Toronto. He made it through security, wandered perfunctorily through duty-free and then headed straight for the Delta

VIP lounge. Oscar told him all about it, but it was so much better in real life: a buffet! Good Wi-Fi and charging stations at every comfortable seat. Even a Nathan's Famous hot dog cart! He was definitely having one of those!

NEW message from Ralph: Oscar, you were right this place is awesome!"

As they don't make actual flight announcements in the lounge, Ralph nervously and regularly checked the departure board, cross-checked the weather and three different flight apps as well as the location of his passport and ticket, which had not moved from his briefcase for more than a week.

Finally, it was time to go. Let me get there before all the overhead space is gone, Ralph thought. Then he remembered he was in business class and not his usual peasant class, and wryly smiled to himself.

After warm greetings from the flight attendants, he settled in after quietly marveling at all the space he had to himself. The hot towel (!) was followed by a dish of warm nuts (!!). Free (and *nice)* noise-canceling headphones (!!!), a meal, despite filling up at the buffet (*and* a Nathan's dog), on real china and 1000 movies to pick from. This was awesome!

NEW message from Ralph: (Selfie-holding-a-glass-of-champagne) "Flying high, buddy!"

Arrival

A ROUTINE TRIP OF A little less than eight (magical) hours, Delta #168 landed thirty minutes early and quickly zipped into a waiting gate. Ralph took a deep, if jet-fueled, breath when he took his first step off the plane and thought to himself "Europe!" He headed for passport control, looking like he knew exactly where he was going but really just followed everyone else.

While waiting for his luggage, Ralph tried to make a quick checklist again of what souvenirs to buy and who for to get it out of the way today early: Mrs. Neumann, of course. Oscar, Tina, even something for Michael, perhaps.

Feeling giddy by properly using *"hola"* and *"gracias"* at passport control, his bag arrived and he jumped into one of Barcelona's black-and-yellow taxis. It was a Citroen – cool! With a stick shift! Damn! It was about a twenty-five minute ride along the coastal ring road, following the Mediterranean, to his hotel. They passed cargo ships with their orange-picker cranes at full throttle. Crossing the street in front of him was a long line of cruise ship tourists, all wearing color-coded kerchiefs, beginning their sightseeing day.

His hotel, "The Serras," was a five-star, Grand Luxe building on the Passeig de Colom, directly across the street from Barcelona's Port Vell and, a bit further along, the Port Olimpic, which was part of the grand restoration of the city in preparation for the 1992 Olympic Summer Games.

As they pulled up in front, Ralph thought "Hey, look at that: there's a Little Caesars pizza place right next door!" He then reminded himself that Super Neumann does not eat Little Caesars, at least not on this trip. No way, Jose!

Unfamiliar with the tipping protocol (which is minimal), Ralph gave an outsized tip to the cabdriver, who thanked him like a long-lost cousin. He checked in, not with the front desk like "ordinary" guests, but with the warm and smiling (and English-speaking) concierge Natalia at the VIP desk. His room was *very* nice, with a super view of the port, the mega-yachts and the palm-tree lined esplanade complete with a kind of cartoon sculpture of a giant lobster. In the distance was a two-stage cable car stretching across the harbor. It was a lot to take in, but take it all in he did.

New SMS from Ralph: "I am *not* rubbing it in, but this is amazing!"

Barcelona is Spain's busiest port, and watching the yachts, ferries and cargo ships sail out of Port Vell toward Genoa, Tunis, and Marseille was a reminder of Ralph's sudden possibilities, at least in the grandest James Bond style. He imagined he could be headed out to a simple dinner in town, then suddenly jump onto the overnight ferry to Tangiers to escape or hunt down his nemesis-du-jour.

After remembering Oscar's advice to resist a nap, Ralph showered, putting on the too-small-but-who-cares hotel slippers and luxuriating in the hotel bathrobe. Hmm I wonder how much this costs? He texted Mrs. Neumann (and Oscar and Tina and Michael to thank them all again) and then went upstairs to the hotel rooftop for a sunny, amazing-view breakfast. Like "everything" he wanted on this trip, his breakfast was authentically "Spanish": *tortilla Espanola*, the egg-potato-onion omelet; some slices of *jamon* and *chorizo* and two *café con leche* coffees. This was *definitely not* a Sheraton! Ralph also caught himself and did not, as per Mrs. Neumann's advice "…take a roll with some cheese and put it in your pocket for later, just in case you get hungry…"

This was gonna be *great*, Ralph quietly exulted to himself. Watch out world: Super Neumann had landed!

Saturday City Stroll

FRESH, CLEAN AND WELL FED, Ralph wanted to walk the city, to smell and sense and feel things, especially in himself, he never knew existed before. He checked in again with the lovely Natalia at the concierge desk and asked about some shopping ideas. With Google Maps and the Citymapper app, he figured he could determine how to get somewhere, if not in a straight line. Natalia mentioned the "Mare Magnum" shopping mall across the street, just in case he might have forgotten something from home, and then directed him to El Corte Ingles, the be-all-and-end-all department store facing Placa de Catalunya.

"Just exit the hotel, turn right and walk until you see the statue of Christopher Columbus. Then turn right again and walk straight up "Las Ramblas" until you reach the end, which is Placa de Catalunya. On your right you will see El Corte Ingles, where you can find anything and everything."

Looking sweetly over Ralph's somewhat portly frame, she also suggested renting a bicycle, but Ralph wanted to walk – maybe he'd even lose some weight on this trip!

"There are many touristic shops along the Las Ramblas, but I don't recommend them. And do be careful and watch out for pickpockets. I guess you are from New York so you know all about that?"

What? Pickpockets? Hmm, well *this* was news to Ralph, though he smiled and scoffed, confidently assuring Natalia of his streetwise preparedness as a native New Yorker, who could spot a scam or a "skell" a kilometer away. But he *did* make note of her admonition and turned up his check-your-back-o-meter.

Wearing his new purchases head to toe, Ralph sauntered out of the hotel with a huge smile and began to swallow in everything he saw and heard along the way.

On his right, he passed a few scooter rental shops; some ragged bars full of crusty old sailors with plastic photos of bad-looking paella flanking the doors; three New York-style "bodegas" (called, oddly enough, "super *mercados*") making note *just* in case he needed to try some new chips. For research purposes only!

There was the grassless and pretty cool-sounding "Placa del Duc de Medinaceli" with old men feeding the birds and young men sleeping in box forts, and the rather-stunning "Basilica de la Merce", Merce being one of the two patron saints of Barcelona (Santa Eulalia is the other, he had read) with a just-married wedding party in the plaza in front taking family photos. How nice!

A bit further along, sure enough, was Christopher Columbus, pointing the wrong way towards America. A small detail, perhaps, but to those in the shipping industry, one slight course deviation means a huge amount of trouble. The grand statue was surrounded by smaller statues of lions, angels and griffins as well as pigeons and tourists getting their picture taken.

Across the street from Columbus was the Customs House and to his right was a government museum with the quirky name of "Engineers, Soldiers and Wise Men". Diagonally across the way was the Maritime Tax authority and the Museum of Maritime History, with quite a display of galleons, sailboats, lifeboats, and all manner of watercraft. With one last look around before he headed up Las Ramblas, he saw the gantry for the Balearic ferries, the imposing W Barcelona Hotel with its sail-like façade and Barcelona's squat version of the World Trade Center.

Las Ramblas was an amazing stretch, about three-quarters of a mile long, of undulating gray and white tiles, with a center strolling area flanked by a single car/bus/taxi/scooter lane on either side. All kinds of stores and restaurants, and touts from both, lined the length of the street. It definitely had a raffish air about it: Ralph almost expected to see three-card monte games in progress. As Natalia suggested, many of these shops were low-end trash-and-trinkets kinds of places, and the accompanying (bad) restaurants with their giant goblets of weirdly colored drinks were totally unappealing. Every city has its tourist zones, Ralph thought, but this was not to his liking. He also did not want to bring back cheap keychains or ashtrays, not matter how colorful they were, as gifts – Super Neumann would not roll like that!

Although it was 1 p.m., there definitely were more than a few shady looking characters along Las Ramblas. Tipped off by Natalia, Ralph simply made note of them. Fortunately it all got MUCH better at the top at the Placa de Catalunya and inside El Corte Ingles.

After shopping and picking up some nice gifts for Mrs. Neumann and some interesting snacks, ("...*just for a taste, that's all*...!) Ralph, feeling a bit emboldened, checked his list of places to eat he had read about that sounded interesting to try.

Caelum – for macarons

El Quim de la Boqueria– in the amazing Boqueria marketplace for some *tapas*

La Cova Fumada – for its famous "*bomba*" which was a strange kind of fried ball of mashed potatoes – a Spanish knish! - with hot sauce on top. *That* might have to wait until tomorrow.

Santa Augustina – for *tapas* in a lovely little plaza which he figured he would never be able to actually find.

Granja La Pallaresa – for hot chocolate and *churros*. That was *definitely* a must-stop on the way back to the hotel.

It was now time for a nap, thought Ralph. While he *was* jetlagged, he also was so keyed up about the city, the trip so far and the whirlwind of the opportunity, he did not fall asleep right away. Setting his alarm, per Oscars instructions, he took a siesta for a few hours and then got himself up and out for more of the city and dinner.

Trying to re-set his clock, he went for another walk, heading to "El Quatre Gats" for dinner. On the way back, he oriented himself towards the hotel, sidestepping the individual-can-of-beer vendors, selfie-stick sellers and guys selling a colored lights thingamajig on a giant rubber band that were surely designed to distract you while your pocket got picked!

Walking back down the Las Ramblas, once Christopher Columbus came into view, Ralph turned left, thinking this was his street, even though it looked darker. Wanting to be sure of himself, but definitely not sure, he walked slowly and carefully along Carrer de la Merce, where he had peeked in on the wedding earlier in the day.

But at night, although Carrer de la Merce was a bit uncomfortable, for Super Neumann, it was much more interesting than pretty much any other street he had walked down in his life: graffitied doorways to dingy apartment hallways lined the block. The gates of shuttered bars that looked like they might have be cool at one time, like La Republica, El Bombon and Bar Celta Pulperia with the cartoon octopus. The light in the distance from the *Bar La Plata* kept him from turning around. That, and the need for Super Neumann to not back down. He gripped the small knife in his pocket and powered on, checking his Citymapper app while being sure to literally watch his back.

He breathed a quiet sigh when he got to the Bar La Plata, which was in the alley next to the Hotel Serras. Wow, he thought, I not only made it, but this place looks cool, and just grungy enough to be interesting too. After all, the hotel was literally across the alley, so if the vibe was weird, he'd just leave for the safety and comfort of his super room, that bathrobe and those too-small slippers. His "emergency snacks" were just waiting to be opened, justifying them as a small reward for not turning tail and finding a brighter street or a taxi. Ralph consciously reminded himself of the steps he *needed* to take outside of his daily life, and along with that sketchy walk, the Bar La Plata looked like just the place to do it.

Not exactly swinging doors with the new sheriff in town busting in, Ralph entered, nodded to the bartender in his version of cool nonchalance, and despite being a very small bar, found a seat.

That night, Ralph learned the soft and hidden power of homemade Spanish-style "*vermut*" and quietly but happily straggled back to his room. The bartender, "Salva" (short for Salvatore) at Bar La Plata was nice and welcoming and spoke enough English to serve Ralph's curiosity. He also served enough *vermut* to melt a good portion of Ralph's brain into a deep sleep.

Never much of a drinker – chips and porn were destructive enough vices – Ralph found *vermut* much to his liking. It was sweet but with a kick he had not initially detected until he did and had to straighten up quick just to walk across the alley.

Although very limited, Ralph played the "all things Spanish" card and along with his (multiple) *vermuts*, had two of the four (and only four!) things on the menu: "*pan con tomate* and a plate of "*butifarra*". He passed on the fried anchovies and sardines. Ralph loved fish but oddly for a "man of the sea" he was not a "fishy fish" kind of guy, though he did think about it, seeing people at pretty much every one of the six tables and the small bar eating them. The *vermut*, however, told him to stick to what he knew, bread and sausage. And this night, the *vermut* would not lie to him.

Sunday Walk to the Fira

SUNDAY WAS INDEED A SUNNY DAY and Ralph thought he should take a walk to get his bearings for the conference. According to the ever-lovely and always-smiling Natalia at the front desk, it was about one and a half miles to the Fira de Barcelona. Armed with a plan, Ralph headed for another superb breakfast on the terrace overlooking Port Vell and sat for a second *"café con leche"* while dreaming about a life onboard the enormous yacht "Lady Moura" parked in the marina in front of the hotel. A fresh shirt, comfy shoes, the new Etnia sunglasses he bought from El Corte Ingles (thanks to the flattery of a lovely and bilingual saleswoman), Ralph was off on a Sunday stroll, bursting with a new and strange sensation of happy confidence.

Stepping directionally out of the hotel, he had only gone to his right as far as the Christopher Columbus statue but now he was headed more or less in a straight line to the trade fair conference center, the Fira de Barcelona and the *Plaza Espana*.

Passing (probably American) joggers along the way, he sniffed at their expensive leisure outfits and determined looks on their faces. It was a nice enough stroll, he thought, but as per Natalia, he had his eyes peeled for something really Spanish. She said you will know you have arrived when you see it! You can't miss it! A bullring!

No, there are no longer bullfights in Catalunya, she explained. They were outlawed many years ago. Now it was a big shopping mall. Disappointed but still thrilled, Ralph saw it and marveled at its tiled façade. A real bullring, he smiled to himself! After seeing its across-the-Plaza proximity to the Fira, he went inside to see all the unfamiliar shops and cool things. So far, pretty much everything about this city was cool to Ralph.

The bullring even offered access to the roof with a grand view of not only the Plaza Espana below and the Fira off to the right, but also the magnificent steps leading up to the National Museum. Further up the hill was the Olympic stadium and assorted facilities left over from the 1992 Olympic Summer Games, which had really put Barcelona on the global map and made it a top tourist destination ever since. The walkway, flanked by two huge entrance columns, was lined with Romanesque statues and from the street level it seemed like "Oz" in the distance.

The bullring, "La Monumental," flanked the Plaza Espana, a grand semi-circle with a stunning fountain – he told himself to remember to go back and watch it at night for the "magical" effects and water ballet. Okay, maybe it wasn't the Bellagio, but it was *not* another conference at the Javits Center in New York either. He stood for a moment to take in all the grandeur, and smiled smugly at the fact that he was not in one of the hotels directly opposite the Fira but in his super spot, with the view of the harbor and the great little bar around the corner. Ralph felt lucky, and privileged and suddenly realized he had never felt either of these two sensations quite possibly ever before. It made him, imperceptibly, puff his chest for the first time in a long, long while.

New message from Ralph: "Dude, Barcelona is beautiful!"

After checking out the Fira, Ralph went back to the bulling shopping mall – every mall has a food court, he thought – to get a small Spanish snack, he hoped, and to maybe look for a souvenir or two. Hey, churros and empanadas! Ralph could barely contain his happiness, absorbing every moment and every inch of being in a bullring across from such a magnificent place as Plaza Espana. It's so European, like Jason Bourne might come screeching around the Plaza at any minute in a souped-up Audi with its bumper dragging sparks, bullets flying and 10 police cars in hot pursuit!

Well, time to slowly return to the hotel, Ralph thought, feeling happy and bold. The return trip, detouring a bit from the walk there due to some street construction, took him through the very pleasant Sant Antoni neighborhood: tidy streets with a small park here and there for the kids. And suddenly, as if he passed some sort of invisible boundary, he came upon the much-funkier Raval neighborhood.

When Ralph crossed the Calle Riera Alta, things literally got dark, both the street and the people. The shops that were "normal" now turned into a series of mobile phone stores, halal butchers and small fruit and vegetable kiosks with a little shawarma stand. The shadows were darker, the street smells more intense and the languages were more, shall we say, intercontinental.

It had gotten "curry in a hurry" (a joke he used to share with Oscar when deciding what to order for take-out lunch.)

Ralph noticed the change quickly. He gripped his phone a bit tighter, making sure he did not stare too long at it lest he take his eyes off the street, in front and especially behind him. Newly confident and empowered, though definitely on edge, he was determined to stand his ground, if necessary. On one hand, it was a sunny Sunday afternoon. On the other hand, very little sunlight penetrated the narrow streets here and by the long looks he got at each street corner, he clearly stood out as a non-native. As a New Yorker, he just moved ahead, expressionless, trying but failing to look like a local. Or at least not like a "pigeon."

Stay cool, stay cool he thought as he tried to gauge which direction he needed to go without staring at his Citymapper app or stopping to look and getting buzzed by a scooter passing *way* too close to him, testing his reaction.

He quickly walked down Carrer de l'Hospitalet, hoping he would not need a hospital before he got back to the hotel. Bit by nervous bit, he made his way and sure enough, reached Las Ramblas and headed towards Christopher Columbus.

Breathing both a bit heavy and sighing with relief, he was never in any actual danger, but he definitely was hearing his own alarm bells to keep his head up and his feet moving. He got back to the room feeling pretty proud of himself, having walked through not exactly the lion's den, but a definite rough spot, and coming out of the other side intact. Super Neumann can do this, he quietly exulted to no one but the mirror. It's time for a celebration drink, he thought, and feeling emboldened and in a Barcelona city groove, went up to the terrace for Sunday happy hour to take in the view from where he had come from.

Posidonia

Posidonia 2022 – Maritime Conference on Port Management, Logistics, Law and Safety, Barcelona. (moved from Athens due to COVID 19)

RALPH WAS UP AND OUT EARLY for day one of Posidonia, looking and feeling sharp. He strode out of the elevator with plenty of time to walk to the Fira.

"Buenas dias, Natalia!" Ralph chirped.

"Hola Sr. Neumann! *Como estas?*"

"Bien, gracias" said the suddenly bi-lingual Ralph. "I'm off to the show!"

"That's great. Enjoy! By the way, here, take a hotel umbrella, it actually might rain today, they say. And don't forget to download the Cabify app. It's much more popular here than Uber, in case you get stuck somehow."

"Oh, wow, *muchas gracias!*"

"De nada Senor Neumann. Have a great day!"

(I'd fuck her, thought Ralph. I wonder if she'd fuck me? Hmm probably not.)

The cargo shipping business had never been a career goal for Ralph. In fact, he'd been generally unsure of what to do with his life, taking odd liberal arts courses here and there, some history classes as well as a graphic arts workshop at Hofstra University. But nothing seemed to really strike him as something he could see himself doing for a career. Chips and porn were not career avenues. He thought about applying for a job with the New York Mets, but the thought of "selling himself" on the phone trying to sell tickets, the usual entry-level job, made him shudder with embarrassment. One day, Mrs. Neumann told Ralph that the husband of one of her mahjongg friends worked at League Leader Cargo, which was not too far from their home and that her friend casually mentioned her husband was having a hard time finding decent people willing to learn a complicated business who were serious and responsible. While Ralph knew nothing about ships or cargo, he did see himself as serious and quietly responsible and in a moment of sad self-reflection, confessed to himself that he needed to do *something*, so why not investigate that business and try it? Maybe it would help get him out of the house, if not permanently, then from 9-to-5 all week long.

Posidonia, named after Poseidon, the Greek god of the sea as well as the prevalent flowering seagrass in the Mediterranean, was the Oscars of the shipping industry and since COVID began, cargo, supply chain, international trade and its transportation were very much in the news. The star of the show these days, intertwined with COVID, was the heretofore lowly shipping container, a simply steel box that allowed anything manufactured "here" to get "there" no matter what it was or where it needed to go. Shipping companies were raking in billions of dollars, taking advantage of the COVID-crisis and charging crazy fees in times of consumer and manufacturer desperation. Although the China-to-Los Angeles/Long Beach route was critical and highly prof-itable, LLC, LLC brokered all kinds of transactions worldwide, from coal and iron ore to Cape Town to bicycles and soybeans to Oostende.

Cargo ships themselves had grown enormously as world trade exponentially expanded. These days, it's common to transport up to twenty thousand containers, each twenty feet long, on a single ship, called a "Neo Panamax vessel." Port slowdowns caused by bad weather, higher fuel prices, a lack of stevedores due to COVID as well as manufacturing lockdowns in China combined to make the cargo business a fascinating industry. Ralph, for once, felt like he was at the center of the universe.

Globalization had turned many industries into "just-in-time" manufacturers and COVID had upended the entire planets shipping expectations. Posidonia had, along with lectures, seminars and presentations, a product fair, showing new kinds of ropes, containers, onboard waste processing, alternative fuels, and all manner of worker products such as waterproof uniforms, heavy duty gloves, non-slip deck boots and thermal underwear. It also showed the daily update of the "Baltic Dry Index (BDI)" which was the global thermometer of freight shipping rates for ships of all sizes. The Index is an average for prices paid for the transport of dry bulk materials across more than twenty common shipping routes. The BDI is often viewed as a leading indicator of the health of global economic activity as changes in the index reflect the supply and demand for key materials used in manufacturing worldwide. High production costs, long lead times, the availability of ships for specific loads and the ever-changing cost of fuel makes the Index an important gauge of global trade.

Fotini

RALPH GOT ON THE POSIDONIA registration line, looking around and around and happily marveling at everything. Suddenly a very attractive woman tapped him on the shoulder and a bit breathlessly asked "Hello, sorry what time do you have? I realize I left my mobile phone in the hotel room!

"Oh sure, its 8:45" said Ralph, flashing his new wristwatch.

"Oh what a nice watch! Sorry! I'm late to meet a colleague, would you mind if I cut in the line with you?"

"No, of course not!" declared Ralph, glaring at the people behind him not to mess up his new found fortune. "Be my guest!" The New Yorker in Ralph sniffed the possibility of some kind of international scam being played on him. They were almost at the front of the line to register, check-in and get the Posidonia welcome goody bag while the woman busied herself searching for something in her bag. Ralph quietly debated if he had just been taken for a sucker – Really? Here? – or if she was legit. She *was* definitely cute so Ralph gave her the benefit of his doubt: the Ralph in Ralph welcomed any advancement of a pretty woman, nefarious or otherwise.

They reached the check-in desk and both stepped forward to one of the lovely hostesses to sign in. Finished and ready for the show, she turned to Ralph, touching his arm gently, and said "Thank you *so* much for your kindness, I really appreciate it! I hope you have a nice Posidonia! Bye for now!"

"Yes you too!" said Ralph, watching her very cute ass fade away, still a bit flustered and now mad at himself that he did not make more small talk with her. Who wants drinking games with Filipinos when this woman was nearby? Oh well.

As Oscar had correctly described, the show was at times genuinely interesting, brutally boring and overall, a festival of shipping horniness, with eyeballs of all shapes, colors and circumferences clicking around every presentation, wondering, hoping, imagining who might be approachable at the lunch area or after-show cocktail parties. Never forgetting the expected report, Ralph took careful notes at each meeting and close-up pictures of products he thought might be of interest to others at LLC, LLC. But he too was also on the prowl and, he was *sure*, exchanged a few smiles and glances with more than one woman. "Me like-y" Posidonia!" thought Super Neumann!

The conference was filled with people from every corner of the world and each attendees badge had a small flag of their home country on it: Iceland, Japan, Chile, France, the Philippines (naturally – there were a *lot* of those) and Greece (surprise!), Russia and Tunisia. It was a fun, harmonious atmosphere and Ralph fell right into the groove of it all, even though he was by himself.

The newness of the first day made things interesting and lunch suddenly became fun, too – Ralph boldly picked out a free seat among a table with Germans, Swedes, Koreans and, to Ralph's sudden delight, *next to the very pretty woman who had cut in line!*

"Well, hello again! Is this seat free?" said Ralph in a very lame attempt at appearing either devilish or charming.

"Oh hello! Yes, please do sit down! Allow me to introduce myself, I am Fotini. From Cyprus."

Ralph's throat clearing ensued. "Oh, hello Fotini from Cyprus, I am Ralph from New York. Very nice to meet you again and, (fumblingstumbling)"*Yiasou!*" Ralph had learned that from some Greek clients who had visited the office and it "worked" when he tried it at a local Greek restaurant. It worked here, too and Fotini's lovely face brightened considerably at Ralph and Ralph's effort.

"What an interesting name you have! Can I ask what the meaning of it is?"

"Oh, thank you. It means "light" or "brilliance." That's very kind of you to ask."

"And how are you (leaning forward to see the name tag), Mr. Ralph? How did you enjoy the show this morning?" Fotini asked calmly, perhaps even sweetly and genuinely while digging into her seafood paella.

"Oh I enjoyed it! This is my first time here at Posidonia so everything is interesting. How about you? Did you find your colleague?" Hey so far so good, Ralph thought!! Glib, relaxed, natural and nothing had spilled on his shirt yet.

"Yes I did, thanks all to you! I've been coming to Posidonia for a few years, but this is my first time in Barcelona actually. All my years in Cyprus but I never made it here before. It's really beautiful!"

"Oh it's amazing! It's my first time, too. It's really special."

A slightly-pregnant pause ensued but Ralph gathered himself and quickly charged to the front of the conversation. He could have asked a thousand questions. "So, how is your hotel?" Maybe awkward, maybe ill-timed, maybe transparent in his state of intrigued horniness, the question nonetheless did not fall flat. Imperceptibly stunned with himself, Ralph was fully at ease with this conversation! Viva Posidonia!

"Actually, my hotel is fantastic, for a few reasons. First of all it's really intimate and super quiet. I find these narrow streets just as bad for noise bouncing off the walls the same as if I stayed on a main street. But *this* hotel is in the *craz*-iest little *corner* of a *tiny* little side-street-off-of-a-side street. It's *so* secluded, which is actually kind of sexy, really, but a bit scary too."

Ralph was *sure* she smiled *at* him when she suggested how sexy the hotel was. He was *almost sure* of it.

"How about you? Are you in one of the hotels around here?"

"No, actually" – holy shit, thought Ralph, she's not only talking with me but seems actually *interested* in *me* – "I'm in a great place too, about two kilometers from here. It faces the harbor."

"Really? I am right near the port as well, just set back a street or two from it. If you are going to the welcome mixer tonight, maybe we can walk back together?"

Alarm bells rang like a DEFCON 1 siren in Ralph's head. *This woman just asked ME out! WTF!!!!!*

"Oh yes, that would be great! I'd love to!" replied Ralph, calm and firm and seemingly used to such banter as this. "I walked here the other day, just to chart my course – sorry, a little shipping humor, so I think I know the way back. I will definitely find you at the party!"

Ralph had taken all of *no* bites of his cannelloni through this mind-bending exchange and realized he had better stuff his mouth before it all went to Ralph-hell.

"I'm giving a lecture on the changing salinity of the world's oceans tomorrow so I will go to the party for just a bit and then go back to the hotel to practice my speech and get a good night's sleep. You don't have to wait for me if you don't want to" she said. Ralph could *swear*, all coy, doe-eyed and utterly removed from innocence, that Fotini knew exactly what his reply would be.

"No, no absolutely I would love to walk back with you. The other day I guess I went down the wrong street on my return and things got a bit funky, oh, um, sorry, a bit scary, though it turned out to be fine. So I promise we will not go *that* way."

"Ha, ha no I know what funky is! I have good cousins who live in Astoria in New York and they taught me so much about American culture when they would come to Cyprus for their summer holidays. 'Funky' is one of those words that can be both bad or good, depending on who says it, how they say and what the situation is, right?"

"Yes, exactly! Well then, I will see you at the party later on! It was lovely to meet you, Fotini!" Ralph suavely said, skidding any potential verbal stumble to a halt.

"The same for me, Mr. Ralph! Enjoy the afternoon!"

New message from Ralph: "YO! I met a very hot woman today! Will explain later."

Ralph watched Fotini walk towards the exit. (I'd fuck her. I wonder if she'd fuck me? Ralph thought. No, probably not.) He noticed much more about her now than he did in the registration line and he quietly shook his head to himself at how genuinely attractive she was, and in more than few ways, his "type." She seemed to glide away, effortlessly but with a determined pace, her cute little ass swinging and swaying.

For all the porn Ralph consumed, he was not a "picky" viewer. Although Ralph would have anyone who would have him, he was generally and genuinely attracted to the gypsy Mediterranean-type: dark eyes, athletic shape, black hair and Fotini was surely and fully that. Petite, with a warmth about her, he fell for that look ever since he knew what girls were and peeked at his neighbor, Maria Tremonti, as often and as surreptitiously as he could.

She also had nice hands, a kind of fetish of his: he liked women with nice hands, delicate, with nice polished nails. A small detail, to be sure, and most certainly not a deal breaker if anyone ever got close enough to Ralph to have their hands on him, but, well, it was his thing, in a way. Not (necessarily) big tits or a big ass, really. Those, though, *certainly* had their place!

Holy cannoli, Ralph thought, *is this happppppeeennnninggggg-gggggg*? Ralph was delusional enough to actually think *something* was (or might be) happening and Super Neumann was DEFINITELY in the house, even if no one else was home! He floated through the rest of the day's lectures, his head on a swivel looking to see if he could "suddenly" cross paths again with Fotini. Always Ralph, he continued to take careful notes for his report, but was completely distracted by his lunchtime encounter. He kept checking to see how long it would be until party time.

If Fotini planned to only stay briefly at the party, Ralph made sure he was on time for the start of it. He positioned himself, "casually" scanning the buffet offerings without an ounce of genuine interest. He didn't want a chive or piece of ham sticking to his teeth before Fotini came, so he just gazed but did not graze. While he glanced down at the offerings, he also kept looking up at the door, watching for Fotini through the throngs.

5:15 – With the room beginning to fill a bit more now. Ralph thought maybe he should go out and go to the men's room or take a short walk to waste some time and appear less eager than the froth on his forehead suggested. Not that Ralph really knew much about party etiquette, but in the small party world of the office breakroom at LLC, he knew only the truest of losers showed up first for the cake, no matter the occasion.

5:35 – With squeaky-clean hands and a spin around the product fair once more, Ralph slipped back inside the party. Trying to appear nonchalant but picturing his "delighted surprise" when he crossed Fotini's path, he got himself a red vermouth, his new favorite drink of suave sophistication. But he drank alone.

5:57 – Excusing himself while slipping between folks laughing, drinking and enjoying each other's company while he wandered the room, Ralph started to get a sensation in his stomach of soul-draining sadness. It was all going so well, *too* well, he thought. "You're an ass, Ralph. Who are you kidding besides yourself?" he thought. Ralph had spent the day thinking of Fotini and not inculcating himself in groups of Greeks or Filipinos, or any other group – what, the Danes don't like to drink? - to set himself up for the party and then whatever mayhem he'd been "promised" would happen afterward. He just *couldn't* go back to the office without a drinking story or three! They'd never let him go back to Posidonia again!

6:23 – No Fotini. Ralph wasn't sure if he should be mad at himself or her. He also considered being mad at nobody at all, but that felt far less satisfying. He wasn't even sure he should be "mad" though "crushed" was locked in a cage match with "mad" and "embarrassed" at that moment. All the good, all the excitement of "Super Neumann" drained from his body and as the crowd began to thin out, groups and no-doubt liaisons, formed over the ninety minutes he stood around like a lonely clown, were leaving for a night of fun. He felt like the cartoon donkey with the lollipop for a head that says "all day sucker" stamped on his ass. Ralph concluded it was time to leave, that Fotini was not going to show up at this point. She was just being nice and he was, as the law of averages (and not the laws of attraction) say, being reverted to the mean: lonely loser again. Maybe it was time – but, damn, so soon? - to fold up Super Neumann's cape and return to "Ralphie boooyy" he miserably thought.

Everything and everyone at Posidonia was an opportunity Ralph had never encountered before. Ralph had googled Fotini to see what she was all about. A leading world class expert on oceanography, tides and the hierarchal food chain of the seas, Ralph thought "Oh boy, stand down on this one. She is *wayyyy* out of your league, Neumann." A masters and two PhD's degrees plus a research fellowship at the Woods Hole Oceanographic Institution left him feeling a bit crushed, but when he looked at his new, sophisticated-looking watch for the hundredth time that morning, he quickly followed that thought with a more determined idea, to *try* and connect again with her. She *did* seem genuinely nice and actually interested in him so let's, for once, not throw in the towel after the first round, he thought encouragingly. But how? When? Where?

New message from Oscar: "Bro what's happening???

New message from Ralph: "Don't ask." Weeping emoji.

Ralph left the party alone. Shuffling sadly and thinking about his route back to the hotel, standing and waving just outside the doors to the Fira were two "mamma mia!" -looking women, laughing and handing out cards of some sort. Half-smiling, Ralph took one, as well as taking the sweet wink from one of the two women, and kept on walking. At the corner (once he had turned around to look wistfully and catch their act again) he checked the card: "Apricots – Trustworthy Call Girls." He slipped the card into his pocket. In cold reality, he was thinking about Fotini and dinner. But he did not throw the card away.

He stopped and considered taking a taxi back to the hotel and either drowning himself at Bar La Plata, or asking Natalia where he should eat – Hey, maybe she would like to join him? Hmmm probably not. He was going out, no matter what, and no matter alone, he thought grimly.

Then, suddenly, a tap on the shoulder and a "Hey, Mr. Ralph!" cracked like thunder! Ralph spun and there was Fotini, out of breath, again, yet beaming, again.

"Oh hey there! I waited for you...."

"No, no Mr. Ralph I'm *so* sorry! They moved my presentation to Wednesday instead of tomorrow so I had to stay with the technicians and stage producer to finalize the look and timing of my speech. I'm *really* sorry I did not make it to the party! And of course I left my mobile phone in the hotel and the organizers would not give me your number, for security, you know. But! But! Did you really wait for me?"

Flustered, elated, confused, elated again, Ralph said "Yes, yes I did, I said I would. But it's okay, I just thought you had much more important things to do and forgot about me." Two could play at the doe-eyed sympathy game, thought Ralph, though knew he was terrible at it. Still, what the heck! In truth he was a bit pissed off, though much more at himself than her.

"No way Mr. Ralph! And here I am, running late again but here I am!"

"Yes, well, since you missed the party, are you hungry? Would you like a drink? I mean, are you busy or rushing back to your hotel now?" Suddenly Ralph was a sweet, innocent devil in disguise. He was also genuinely hungry.

"Yes, yes and no! But do you know a place around here or somewhere we could go?"

"Actually, I passed a place that looked good and very "local" on my way back the other day. The street is kind of funky – hey there's that word again! – but it will be okay, I'm sure." Ralph slyly double-checked his pants pocket for the small fish-shaped knife he brought with him after the sudden change of street vibe the other day. "I think I have the card here", he said, fishing through his goodie bag. "Here it is: *"Bar Muy Buenas"* How bad could a bar called 'very good bar' be? And if it's awful, I passed another good place for tapas, which we must have, no?"

Brimming with heretofore unknown confidence, the mercury of his mood swung from freezing to boiling in about three seconds.

"Great! Let's go! I'm very happy to have found you! I thought 'Oh there is no chance he waited for me. He probably forgot all about me!' "

"No, no, I am a man of my word. Of course I waited. I thought *you,* high powered oceans-expert that you are." forgot about *me.*

"Ha ha! Who are you talking about, me? Nooooo not really, but thank you" Fotini purred and flashed a sweet smile.

"But wait, do you prefer to take a taxi? Your heels are quite lovely but maybe you prefer not to walk?"

"Mr. Ralph, I am a woman, born with heels on! No way, let's walk! I will get to see a bit more of this beautiful city." Ralph gulped with delight and off they went.

In the limited time he had been in Barcelona, Ralph was in a constant state of marvel, not only at his good fortune, but at the beauty of the city. Every building, it seemed, had some kind of remarkable architectural detail. The pace of things was definitely "big city" but without the inherent, unruly madness of New York. Ralph found himself at ease and in his own small way, allowed himself to "feel" a tiny bit European and stroll with a casual smile in this sunny place to the soundtrack of the bing-bong-bing of the ambulances, the non-English chatter of Las Ramblas and the putt-putting of the million motor scooters taking off from the red light.

Strolling along – *Ralph was strolling in Barcelona with a beautiful woman!* - a guy on a scooter suddenly shot in front of them, causing Fotini jump back and grab Ralph's arm to wrap hers around it for protection. It was a sudden, genuine, impetuous movement that made Ralph blush and swoon simultaneously. He instinctively touched her hand in comfort and security. All of a sudden, Ralph became a bold protector of little women!

They looked and laughed at each other. "Ooh! What a jerk!" they exclaimed!

"Stupid kids! They are just like that in Cyprus too!" Fotini said. Then they returned to form, walking again just side by side, but the bubble had been punctured by her touch. A line crossed. A new dimension entered. Ralph was imperceptibly dizzy. "Keep it together man!" he screamed at himself!

As they walked – Ralph floated, actually – Ralph asked Fotini the "So, tell me all about yourself, Fotini," question. He also headed off, even temporarily, the reverse question about himself and the empty "nothing-special" reply he had to offer. The table would surely turn at some point, but for now, he wanted to immerse himself in her.

"Me? Hmmm well, I don't know, I'm not very interesting, I think! Where should I begin?

"Ha, I disagree! Begin at the beginning, as they say" said Ralph, hoping she would leave a trail of verbal breadcrumbs that he could follow when it was his turn.

"Well I was born in Cyprus, but you know that. I have lived all my life there. Have you ever been? No? Well it's lovely but a bit boring, really. It did have its wild and dangerous times when the Turks invaded in 1974 and stole half our country, still to this day! I had an older sister who died during the war when we could not get the proper medicine for her. No other brothers or sisters, and so my father taught me everything about the sea and shipping as he had no one else to leave the business to."

"We have some spectacular beaches and I have always loved to swim in the waters so I naturally absorbed all he had to share and took my studies deeper into the oceans."

"I became more interested in academics than shipping and got my masters and two PhD's along the way."

"Ha, ha, I don't want to sound like a Tinder profile, but I enjoy all kinds of music, food and people, except Turks!"

"So how about you, Mr. Ralph?" They arrived at Bar Muy Buenas and took two seats in the back. Thankfully the waiter gave them English-language menus. Fotini ordered a white wine and Ralph, a small Spanish beer, Estrella Damm, along with calamari with artichokes, some *bunuelos de bacalao* and *croquetas de jamon*. All the while Ralph's mind spun, trying to juice his story as quickly as he could. He was petrified this entire encounter was about to implode when he revealed barely a single interesting thing about himself.

"Me? Well I wish I had as exotic and as accomplished a story as yours!" Compliments to keep the fire glowing, he thought. "I am born and raised on Long Island in New York. To be honest I kind of backed into my job, but I enjoy it very much. Many things in life do not follow according to plans, I guess. I've been there twelve years already."

"I like sports, mostly baseball but I'll watch pretty much anything on TV. I also like different foods, especially spicy things (this was a complete lie, but an attempt to be manly). I've traveled to the Caribbean and I've been to Toronto, too. And I own my own house, so I am becoming a kind of expert in painting, plumbing, gardening and even a (very) little cooking!" (oh, you own your own home in New York – impressive, no?)

"Oh wow, Mr. Ralph that sounds great! You were being very modest!" Blushing, Ralph smiled sweetly at her sweet smile and they both flushed a nice shade of red.

Things seemed calm between them, so Ralph thought it might be the moment to peel back a layer: other than the evil eye necklace and a small tattoo of two dolphins with stars for eyes on her left wrist, he didn't see what could be interpreted as a wedding ring or other tokens of love.

"So, if it's not too personal: Are you married with kids? Sorry if that seems sexist or cliché." Ralph knew this was a probably too blunt and too early to ask, but also thought he needed to seize the conversation. He saw this as a major moment of truth and prayed so hard his butt clenched.

"No, no not at all. No, not married and no kids. You might say I am married to my work." Ralph sighed deeply with relief but also tried to interpret her facial expression along with the statement: was she sad and downcast? Happy and carefree? Wistful? Trepidatious or a swinging single?

"How about you?" Fotini had, in fact, looked to see if he too had a ring of any significance.

"Oh me? No, no one special in my life." Well *that's* out of the way now, Ralph thought. Hmm I wonder if it's out of the way for her, too.

"So we are kind of work-aholics, eh?"

"You might say that, though these past few days have been really fun, exploring Barcelona and being at my first Posidonia!"

"Mmm, these *tapas* are very good. I like the cod the better of the two, but both are good. Good choice Mr. Ralph!"

Beaming, Ralph said "Well, in the Spanish tradition (Ralph read about this cultural nugget in a guide book) shall we move on to the next round of tapas and drinks? There is another place I passed that looked great, though, as they say, you can't eat the atmosphere. Shall we?"

"Yes, we shall!" said Fotini, with genuine glee. "Let me run to the ladies room for a moment?" Fotini saw this night lengthening in a sweet, unthreatening way, so she wanted to "fix her face" for the walk to the next spot.

Ralph took the moment to pay the bill and waited at the table, proud and happy to say the bill was all taken care of.

New message from Ralph: "Back on track!" Two fire emoji.

"Oh, no Mr., Ralph, let me pay my share!" offered the faux damsel-in-distress.

"Absolutely not, the pleasure is all mine" said Ralph, his confidence at an all-time high.

It had gotten darker by now, though there was still a warm glow to the Mediterranean sky. For some reason, Fotini turned left when they exited Bar Muy Buenas, and Ralph instinctively and a bit more firmly than gently, touched her shoulder to spin her around. "It's this way, Fotini."

"Okay Mr. Ralph, lead the way!" She very briefly put her arm in his - again! - to offer her own tender moment that Ralph did *not* ignore.

"Was this the street you said was 'funky?'?"

"Yes, but it will be fine. Remember, I'm from New York!" Ralph quietly panicked at the thought of being a fake big shot should, God forbid, anything *actually* happen to them in the street. But memories of "One Punch Neumann" let him stride with (some) confidence.

They both laughed and their fleeting moments of shared touches felt very comfortable, though new for both of them.

"I'm very happy to be here Mr. Ralph. I work a lot and, well, I don't socialize so much. Less than I would like to, but the academic world is not a very social one. Nor does it have, generally, people I could have fun with. I hope that does not sound too cold? I'm not cold, just the opposite! But I am also busy and, I must confess, much more shy than that crazy woman who cut in line in front of you today!"

"I'm very happy to be here too, Fotini. I'm thrilled to be at Posidonia, but being anywhere alone, well, things are always so much more fun when you are with nice people to share things with."

"And speaking of fun, I still have to find a group of Filipinos or Greeks to drink with or they will never let me hear the end of it back in my office!" Ralph laughed.

"Greeks? I can introduce you to all the Greeks here. For better or for worse, their after-show drinking parties *are* legendary. I don't stay long at them, but I'd love to bring you to one. I can protect you there, like you have been doing for me tonight," Fotini said with a sincere smile. "I might be small, but I am tougher than I look. Shipping is a man's world, clearly, but I don't back down" Fotini declared, not as a warning but as a proud declaration.

"Whoa, will I need protection from the Greeks? Oh boy, what goes on at these parties?" Ralph laughed. "I look forward to that!

"So let's see where this place is" mused Ralph. "I know it was in front of this amazing building, a concert hall: the Music Palace."

Ralph remembered the place after leaving El Corte Ingles and had gone left when he exited instead of right and back down Las Ramblas. He ended up on Via Laietana and while waiting to cross at a red light he saw the corner of the Palau de Musica Catalana and walked the fifty yards to see it up close.

It was a stunning building! He took some pictures of it to show his mother. Then he turned to continue south, roughly sensing the direction of the hotel, and when he did, he saw a sign hanging over an elaborate wrought-iron entrance to a very cool-looking bar, "El Bixto." He peeked inside – it was small and intimate – and had an immediate pang of sadness as it seemed too nice and maybe even romantic to enter alone. But the place was really interesting and the sign said "We speak seven languages here" so he made note of that. Who knows, maybe he would go back? Happy though he was with *Bar La Plata*, this place just vibed so cool that while his first thought, as usual, was "I'm not cool enough for this place" his second thought was "hmm let me get a card from this place."

It turns out that the owner was sitting on a stool outside having a cigarette. When he smiled and leaned in to read the posted menu, she smiled and said" Hello! Come in, have a drink."

"Oh, um, no I was just looking at the menu. Ah, you speak English" said a flustered Ralph.

"Yes and many other languages, too. Let me get you a card." She slipped inside and returned. "What event are you here for, or are you a day tourist off a ship, perhaps?"

"Posidonia, actually. It begins on Monday. It's a big meeting about everything in the shipping and cargo industry. Well, thanks! I plan to return!" Ralph said, waving the card, with a less than a fifty-fifty chance of actually doing so but rather thrilled with this exchange.

"Okay, great, yes hope to see you! Nice sunglasses, by the way!"

Even the tiniest of innocent interactions with a smiling woman gave Ralph fodder to dream. That's how and why he bought those expensive Etnia sunglasses at El Corte Ingles – the saleswoman played him into a puddle.

"Oh gracias! I just purchased them at El Corte Ingles! (I'd fuck her. I wonder if she'd fuck me, Ralph thought. No, probably not.)

Ralph nearly skipped down the street after that.

"Yes, here it is. I passed it the other day and it looked very nice and the menu was quite interesting."

They entered and Ralph immediately saw the smiling owner and smiled back. "Hey, nice to see you again!" she said, making Ralph feel like a regular.

"Yes you too. I told you I would come back!" Hmm, thought Fotini, that's the second time this guy kept his word. Interesting.

They snuggled into a small table. "What would you like to drink? What might you like to try, maybe?" the owner asked.

"Fotini, another white wine or would you like to switch to something else?" said Ralph.

"Yes, I prefer white wine myself" she said.

"Great, let me give you a taste of one of my favorites, a Spanish wine, *Xarel.lo*. And for you sir??"

"I'll try a Spanish red!"

"A *Garnacha* for you then. I'll be right back. Here is a menu and there are specials on the mirror over there."

Both wines were delicious. Naturally, they ordered fish dishes to share. The *tapas* were correctly described as *"tapas a-tipicas"* and were all delectable, especially the unusual salmon marinated in coffee, the *"boquerones,"* (which in a hundred years the "old" Ralph would *never* had tried) marinated in Riesling and dill and oxtail with "trumpets of death" mushrooms. Ralph was so proud of himself and his stomach. The whole night of discovery was purely magical.

Ralph was floating in another galaxy but somehow managed to hold his own in conversation, keeping things light but also asking more about Fotini to show interest, which was increasingly genuine and not as prurient as was his normal, and rare, level of female interaction. Fotini shared herself too, though it was a bit edited as she took things step by step.

"I enjoy academia, but I will admit it also saved me from the macho world of shipping, in a way. I learned to 'fight' or, as they say, 'stand my ground' early on, both from watching my father and his negotiations as well on my own, with arrogant Greek boys growing up and arrogant Greek men later on. Academics was fascinating and enjoyable and I did not have to deal with the harassment that comes with a pretty woman in a man's world. Despite the cultural pressure from my family, I never felt the need for a man for any "thing": happiness, children, none of the usual things."

"I do miss my father, though, very much, for so many things. I guess all girls do, as boys feel with their mothers, no?"

Ralph laughed. "Well, I *am* my mother's son, that's for sure, and she never lets me forget it, either!" Uh, oh! Ralph quickly wished he could have retracted that "momma's boy" quip, but at least he laughed enough to deflect the misery of his comment.

He hoped.

They decided it was getting a bit late, though not by Barcelona standards. With the bill happily paid again and with a warm goodbye from the owner – two women nice to him in the same night! – Ralph asked if she wanted to take a taxi. Fotini declined, but when they exited "El Bitxo," to the right was a dark and narrow street. Romantic perhaps at another time, they voted to walk on the main thoroughfare of *Via*

Laietana. The small streets looked enticing, but also had the possibility of being deserted and hence, potentially confusing and then, potentially dangerous. Never a gambler, Ralph decided not to push his luck and chose to walk on the busy, well-lit street.

At the end of Via Laietana, just before the corniche that passed in front of his hotel, was a small back street that led to the tiny further-back street of Fotini's hotel. This was definitely a dark street, and though he could see the light of the Bar La Plata ahead, Fotini stiffened just a bit and tugged on the strap of her purse as they made a right turn onto it.

"Oh my, this is a very dark street!" she said.

"Yes, but don't worry, we are quite close to your hotel, no? We'll be there in a minute or two."

Not wanting this amazing night to end, either in a disaster or otherwise, Ralph made note of a group of young teens hanging out ahead. He took Fotini's hand, in a stunningly bold move for him, to steer her around and away from them, exchanging the toughest glance he could muster that he hoped said to them: back off. Not us.

Breathing a quiet sigh of relief, Ralph rolled the dice one more time that night. "My hotel has a fabulous rooftop bar that overlooks the water. Would you like a nightcap?"

"Oh Mr. Ralph I really shouldn't but thank you so much. But maybe tomorrow?" Fotini was not coy or evasive, but polite and still letting things unfold at *her* chosen pace. Ralph momentarily kicked himself for pushing things too far, but hey, everything else was going great up until then.

Further along was indeed an even darker alcove of a street, Carrer de Riudarenes. "Here we are – crazy, no?" said Fotini.

"Wow, this IS secluded" exclaimed Ralph.

They stopped at the front door of the Wittmore Hotel and faced each other, both of them buzzing with an intrigue that had built all night long, though for Ralph, all day long too.

"Mr., Ralph, I have to say how I much I enjoyed tonight and how much I appreciate what a gentleman you have been, from letting me cut in front of you this morning to the whole evening. I hope we can meet tomorrow so I can return your kindness."

"Fotini, it really was my pleasure to have met you and I can't tell you how much I have enjoyed your company tonight. This was *so* much better than anything I would have done alone, which would have been to eat badly and drink heavily!"

"So shall we make a plan for tomorrow?" Fotini asked with more than a dash of hope?

This was like music sung by legions of angels for Ralph.

"Yes definitely! Do you want to go to the show together in the morning? Or just find each other during the day?" Ralph immediately bit his lip, sensing he just looked pathetic and unmanly by not *making* a plan.

"Let's see! Let me send some emails about meetings I have tomorrow, and their timing, and I will text you before I go to sleep."

"Great! Operators are standing by to take your call" Ralph smirked, then realized what a lead weight of a pun he offered from U.S. late night TV. "Um, I mean SMS".

"Wonderful! Well, good night Mr. Ralph, and thank you again for a wonderful evening." Both heads leaned forward for a welcome and honest two-cheek kiss. Ralph culturally stopped for a nanosecond after the first but he quickly saw the second one coming and recovered in time. He definitely sensed Fotini was not pecking like a hungry chicken to get out of there: those kisses were slow and determined, even for cheeks.

"Good night Fotini. I will wait for your texts."

"Good night Mr. Ralph and thanks again. I will contact you shortly."

Fotini slipped into the revolving door and Ralph rocketed off for galaxies unknown. He turned and walked back towards his hotel, and came upon that same group of guys again. Ralph stared straight ahead, but felt their stare and one of them, slightly older than the others, stepped towards him, ostensibly to throw his cigarette into the street but making Ralph sidestep him awkwardly. Ralph, emboldened by love, gave him a short, hard stare, followed by a shake of his head. He knew that was no innocent move by the guy: he just got tested. The guy made some kind of comment Ralph did not understand and another of the group whistled and shouted "eh..eh...eh"...Ralph kept on, comfortable that he'd returned fire with that look, but not waiting even one more second to see what might happen next.

After all, he had a date tomorrow!

He had just turned the corner at the Bar La Plata and briefly considered a celebratory nightcap vermouth when his phone buzzed. The screen said "Fotini." Oh no, what happened, was she blowing him off already? It had barely been two minutes since they said goodnight? Ohh fuck noooo, please, am I about to get dumped?

"Hey there, hello! Is everything okay?" said the newly appointed head of the "Fotini Protection Agency."

"Yes, yes, hi, everything is great! You are so sweet to ask! So how is that super rooftop terrace of yours for breakfast? I decided to start the day with you instead of another meeting. Is that good for you?" Fotini nearly purred.

A cough and a gasp quickly followed with an excited "Yes, sure! It's really nice there. Oh, so, well, um, this is great! When do you want to meet? I will secure a table for us!"

"Well then, see you at eight! Good night Mr. Ralph"

"Yes, yes, good night Madame Fotini!" Ralph then bee-lined to his room and flopped on the bed to just revel in the entire night. He then stood in front of the full length mirror, raised his fists like Rocky and shouted *"Are you fucking kidding meeee?????"* Unlike when he'd quietly dance in his bedroom at home, Ralph danced around the room in a state of giddiness he had never felt before. Sheer joy made him almost shake with glee and he thought "Holy shit I gotta tell Oscar about this!" When things were "good" for Ralph, it meant, basically, the absence of "bad", like sickness or a car accident. Or his everyday life. Things were *very* good for Ralph right about now, better than they have ever been, which immediately put Ralph in a panicked state of doom, thinking surely *something* was about to go wrong. It just had to. But until it did, Ralph kind of held his head in his hands and said in equal measures incredulously and confidently "Damn, a beautiful woman likes me!"

New message from Ralph: "Dude you will NOT believe it! I don't!"

He quickly set the alarm for 6.00 a.m. to make sure he was up, fresh and ready for whatever lay ahead of this now magical, mystical tour. He should have been wired tight but was so emotionally drained he fell asleep in his clothes when he laid down after the see-you-at-breakfast phone call and slept like the most contented man in Barcelona.

Many people in life are haunted by their failures: Ralph was a hostage to his lack of success. At times it consumed him like he consumed his chips and his porn. For the first time in his life, Ralph felt truly successful, yes, even by this narrow definition.

Ralph was up at 5:15 the next day, excited as he was for the day to begin and petrified he might oversleep and blow the whole thing.

Freshly shaved, clean, a new, Spanish brand "Cruyff" polo shirt, he felt crisp and ready and paced the room for half an hour planning, thinking, wondering, hoping and swimming in an unknown ecstasy.

He quickly raced downstairs first to consult with Natalia about a cozy, dark, maybe even romantic place for dinner, then bolted upstairs to snag a prime table overlooking the yachts and away from the buffet, the juice bar and the noisy coffee machine.

And then he waited. But unlike the party, Fotini did not disappoint and arrived at 8:03 looking fit, smartly styled, beaming and just plain beautiful.

"*Kalimera* Fotini!" Ralph exclaimed. "*Ahhhhhhhhhh muy buenas dias Sr. Ralph!*" as they laughed delightedly with each other. Breakfast was a culinary afterthought, but "café con leche" were still necessary. They did the "morning after" without the actual "after" of anything, with "How-did-you-sleep?" "All-ready-for-another-fun-day-of Posidonia?" chatter interspersed with questions that arose from the processing of the night before.

Fotini suddenly launched into a revelation that would nearly knock Ralph off his chair. With the sun shining on them both, she nonetheless lifted her sunglasses to look directly at Ralph, who actually read the cue, after about thirty seconds, to lift his as well.

"I'm going to tell you something Mr. Ralph: I did not go directly to sleep last night. I was awake, replaying the funfunfun night we had, the delicious food and wine and your company. And then I "talked" to my father about you."

"Really? Uh oh" Ralph blushed, not sure to be honoured or dive under the table for cover.

"Yes, yes, in a very good way. I live my life very much alone, by my own choice. I don't have the patience for silly things or silly, much less stupid, people. No Facebook or Tik Tok nonsense. I work, I study,

I analyze and I spend a lot of time chasing money, for research grants to continue to work, which I really love. I also talk to my father every night, for the things a daughter needs: love and guidance, protection and affection."

"I told him what a great night I had with a very, very nice man, who was very respectful and who protected me in moments I certainly could have managed, at least I think so, but was grateful to have you close by. Who did not ask or expect or require anything of me but my presence."

"That's absolutely true, Fotini. I sincerely enjoyed your company. And I confess, like you, I haven't had an evening like that in, well, I can't even remember."

"My father smiled at me and nodded, in his sweet way, and sends his thanks to you for watching over his princess. And I thank you, too, Mr. Ralph."

"No, no, thank *you* Fotini. Really and truly." Ralph blushed even deeper than before and gulped the last bit of his coffee before he said anything dumb and burst the moment. Hot damn, he thought, I made it into the nightly father conversation!

Ralph was genuinely thrilled to being called "Mr. Ralph." He was sure it was not because an internationally sophisticated woman such as Fotini could not pronounce "Neumann" but took it as a sign of respect, of comfort. After all, her last name was *"Eleftheriou"* so "Neumann" was a piece of cake (or in her case, spinach pie!) in comparison! Could it have been a flirt? Maybe it was just a playful joke with nothing behind it. But maybe not, thought Ralph. Maybe it really was as sweet and endearing as he hoped it was.

Breakfast finished, Ralph said "Well, it's time to go. Do you think we have enough time to walk or should we get a taxi?"

"Let's walk. I enjoy that very much."

As they left the hotel and started towards the Fira, their walk was a mixture of quiet smiles, raging inner thoughts and casual chatting. At one point, waiting at a red light – Ralph remarked how "obedient" Spanish people are waiting for the light to change, unlike the chaos of New York – Fotini said "You know, there are so many beautiful and artistic designs and things to see on every corner here and I noticed these paving stones on many streets. They are really great!"

"Oh, that's so funny: I noticed the same thing when I first arrived and took my first walk. I asked my friend the concierge about it and she said "Yes, these are called 'panots', the rose of Barcelona.'"

"Really a lovely symbol."

Once at the Fira, they gently hugged and did a sweet Euro-double cheek kiss goodbye, agreeing to meet at some point later in the day. Fotini had confirmed her lunch meeting so the plan was to, as they laughed, try to "accidently on purpose" bump into each other during the day, and then meet again at the after-party.

"If it's alright with you, I made a reservation for dinner tonight at an unusual place. Well, not unusual in a strange way, but, I was assured, in a very nice way."

"Most definitely, Mr. Ralph – care to give me a hint about the cuisine?"

"No! It will be, I hope, a delightful surprise! Wait, you're not allergic to anything, are you? Everyone seems to have an allergy of some sort these days?"

"No, not at all. I don't care much for Indian food, but even so, I'll enjoy it with you. Well then, ooh I will be thinking all day about our night. See you later!"

"Yes, ciao for now!" It was the first time Ralph ever said the word "ciao" before. "I'm so fucking continental!" he exclaimed to himself!

The day both dragged achingly slowly and flew by for Ralph, watching the clock, thinking about the night to come and reminding himself to pace himself. Go slow, dammit. Try not to anger Fotini's father with a stupid, impetuous and selfish action. He was, most definitely, horny, but also trying to balance an actual and growing, if possibly misplaced, sense of affection for Fotini.

As they failed to run into each other during the day, 5:00 pm finally arrived and Ralph excitedly hit the after-party. He found Fotini in the middle of a boisterous group of Greeks and Chileans and stood a bit outside the circle, angling himself to get noticed.

"Hey Mr. Ralph, come join us!" Fotini shouted. Smilingly, Ralph slipped into the circle of now-wary men, seeing this potential interloper of their evening fun be greeted so warmly by her. Fotini introduced Ralph in Greek and weak smiles followed with a few head nods and limp handshakes.

After a bit of small talk, the group physically and dynamically shifted, leaving Ralph to say "Am I missing a legendary drinking party?"

"Ha! Maybe, but wouldn't you rather an evening with me?" Uff, there's that doe-eyed charm again, Ralph thought, knees shaking and heart racing.

"Without a single doubt!"

"So to repay your kindness, I asked at my hotel for a place for a drink and another tapa and they gave me a few recommendations. Two of them are right across from each other. Shall we try one and then move on to your secret 'unusual' place?"

"Yes let's!" said Ralph. "I'm ready for all things new, but my kindness does not need to be repaid, Fotini."

"I know this Mr. Ralph, but still, let me invite you. Please?"

"I accept!"

They headed for a bar called "El Xampanyet" but it was clearly packed to overflowing when they arrived and, to Fotini's mind, with a line of pure tourists blocking the street outside it. Okay *they* were tourists too, but still, she thought. So they turned and just a few steps away was a bar, also crowded but accessible, called "Tapeo."

Drinks and some very delicious tapas ensued. It was a boisterous happy hour and their vibe, instead of wearing off or wearing thin, got better and better. Walking to the bar, they had an easy conversation, like old friends, putting smiles on both of their faces. As Fotini had "said" to her father, they were seemingly happy with each other's presence. Neither seemed to be angling (outwardly anyway) for something else; it was all genuine. For Ralph this was a major mental departure, but he went with it, acquiescing to the mood and not wanting to blow the whole thing by being overly horny, which he was. Maybe something would happen, maybe not, but it definitely was a lot better than his usual life: alone.

The Filipinos could wait: he wanted to be with this Greek and this Greek only. Michael and the rest of LLC would just have to understand.

For Fotini, it was a wonderful social departure. Being very attractive but very serious and smart did not always make for a winning social combination, at least not in Cyprus, and she was often both on the defensive of unwanted advances and "alone" in her banal conversations with handsome but not-too-bright men. So she limited her social life rather than lower her standards. She was lonely and the price to be paid for that resulting loneliness took its own toll.

Ralph calculated the travel time to the secret dinner and said "so, shall we move on?"

"Oh yes, I'm so excited! Tell me again it's not Indian food?"

"Ha! No. It's unusual, but I really hope you will enjoy it. I trust Natalia, the concierge in my hotel, and she said you will surely enjoy it."

Fotini insisted on paying for Tapeo, despite Ralph's gentlemanly protestations, and off they went.

A few wrong turns and then down a literal dark alley was the battered wooden door of "La Carassa." Inside was a warren of candlelit alcoves, antiques, lace tablecloths and fondue pots! It was like crossing a transom into a completely different and yes, even romantic, world.

Fotini gasped. "Wow Mr. Ralph! This place is wonderful!"

"I did say it was unusual and I hope you like fondue?" asked Ralph, praying hard she said yes, was not lactose intolerant and already thinking how to thank Natalia for this idea.

"Oh yes, yes I do. This is *so* different! How great!" Ralph beamed with delight at her delight.

They shared a salad to begin followed by an evening bordering (and occasionally trespassing over the border) on romance, along with laughs, cheese, wine, unspoken thoughts, and a shared chocolate mousse for dessert. Ralph could barely contain his happiness at hitting this home run of a night, and at the awe-inspiring past few days of his life.

He sensed in himself a mental metamorphosis he never imagined could be possible. Never. Yet, the spectre of disaster, in one hundred forms, still loomed. Not enough had changed about Ralph's thinking to stop *being* Ralph and his fears of impending doom lingered.

She did not need to be perfect for him. His bar was set quite low and she had leapt over it, in heels no less, the moment she cut in front of him on that line. Was he perfect for her? Not a chance, Ralph feared, but he figured he'd go with the flow until she ultimately tired of him and he returned to his regularly scheduled life. But as he and Oscar used to say "Hey man, *every* dog has its day!"

Given his poor personal frame of reference, Ralph did not know what, exactly, was happening here between them. He prided himself on his New Yorker's sense of bullshit and he detected none of it from Fotini. Fotini, from the rough-and-tumble world of Cypriot shipping and the shady Russian money laundering invading Cyprus, prided herself on being able to quickly read someone's (dis) honest intentions and all she got was a green light from Ralph. She definitely sensed their "loneliness" compatibility. Though his work did not dominate his life and his career was less laudatory than hers, he was honest and sincere, which for Fotini overrode pretty much everything else in a man. Ralph seemed just so…nice. Unpretentious. Genuinely sweet. All things she liked admired and wanted in a man, in any capacity, and nearly impossible to find in the macho Mediterranean. Was he perfect for her? Probably not, though she allowed that there was much more to uncover about each other. But at this stage of life, did it matter? She thought she had found "perfect" partners once or twice before, only to be shown the error of her ways by their handsome-but-unstoppable arrogance. Fotini never lowered herself or her standards for a quick, cheap fuck. Never.

"Well, this was something really special Mr. Ralph!" Fotini exclaimed as they finished the last sips of wine and prepared for the walk back to their hotels.

"I'm really so glad you enjoyed it. I definitely did. I hate for it to end but you have a big presentation tomorrow morning so we should get going, no?"

"Yes, yes, they gave me a prime time spot, 11:00 a.m. on the closing day, before the grand summation and the annual "looking ahead" speech from the organizers. I'm quite excited actually."

Ralph checked his walking app for the route back, and impulsively extended his arm, for the very first time in his life, for Fotini to take. Without a moment of hesitation, she slipped hers inside his and off they went.

The way back was better lit and less charming than the way to La Carassa, Nonetheless, Fotini's arm was in Ralph's, so what could be more romantic? A kiss goodnight, a real kiss goodnight, they both thought. It was time for that.

Down Via Laietana, they turned right onto Placa de Angel, turned again at Placa San Jaume, turned again down Carrer de la Ciutat. The night had been a dream for them both, including this soul-stirring, arm in arm stroll. They turned finally onto Carrer d'en Gignas. The Hotel Wittmore, on Carrer de Riudarenes, a vest pocket of a shoe box, was a bit further along.

Up ahead, in front of a barber shop oddly still open at this hour, was another groups of young guys hanging out, smoking and drinking. Ralph immediately took Fotini's hand and placed hers in his. He wanted a direct grip and she took it, willingly, intertwining her fingers. Tightly. Ralph's chest puffed a bit bigger as they slowly approached the group on the way to Fotini's hotel. Ralph quickly double-checked his left pocket for his small knife but kept a steady pace while his heart began to race.

Over the past few days and nights, Ralph had become a changed man, wholly and completely, from head to toe, inside and out. No longer did he fret about making a mistake of any kind with Fotini, or even allowing himself the possibility of inviting a disaster just because he was Ralph Neumann. So Ralph was going to carry on, if not charge into the breach ahead, and not think (more than) twice about it.

Suddenly the older man who had exchanged a snort and a stare with Ralph the other night emerged from the barbershop and locked eyes with Ralph.

Ralph retuned the stare. He had no choice, really. This night was *not* going to go wrong, Ralph decided then and there.

Ralph actually pulled back just a tiny bit on Fotini's hand to slow their stroll – he did not want to seem like he was "head-down-and-rushing" through this gauntlet, but striding, head up, in command and as fearless as he possibly could look to be.

With Fotini on his right, they passed the group on the left. Another cigarette flew toward Ralph's feet and a guttural laugh came from inside the circle of guys. Quick glances shot from both of them but Ralph and Fotini kept walking. It was at least another thirty yards to her hotel.

Though difficult to see in the dark, Ralph flushed red, half angry at the guys trying to show him up in front of Fotini and half with the rush of adrenaline suddenly coursing through him. "Fight-or-flight" was in full effect but Ralph held his stare, his ground, the small knife in his left pocket and Fotini's hand with his right.

Thinking they were in the clear but not wanting to turn around, they continued on, silent but relieved. Then, within about ten steps of their passing and in total silence, a hand suddenly tugged hard at Ralph's wrist while two guys grabbed Fotini and held her arms.

"*Hey*! Ralph! RALPH!" screamed Fotini. Despite having just passed them, the group had snuck up on them silently and shocked them both. Ralph instantly went from completely relieved to utterly confused to furiously outraged and began to struggle with the one guy pulling on his wristwatch while from the corner of his eye he could see Fotini trying to pull herself away from the other two guys.

"I'll kill you! I'll fucking kill you!" Ralph half-sputtered and half-screamed, words he had never, *ever* used in his life before. Adrenaline burst through his veins like a broken fire hydrant. The band on his new Nixon watch was a bit loose, so he had almost uncomfortably overtightened it to the last hole – he didn't like it jangling on his wrist - and hence made it almost impossible to yank off. Trying to break free and protect Fotini, Ralph suddenly turned from her and to the now-two guys yanking on his wrist. That watch just would not come off.

Ralph would recall later that Fotini was screaming in anger, not fear. Ralph shook one guy off with a hard elbow to his chest and grabbed the other by the neck with his free right hand, pushing him against the wall.

"Hey! HEY MOTHERFUCKER!"

He then twisted his left hand free enough to grab the knife. Unbeknownst to Fotini, Ralph had opened the blade at the corner of Carrer d'en Gignas when he saw how dark and narrow the street had become. The guy he pushed off tripped, fell and then ran off but the other, an odd red-haired guy in a group of Maghrebi-looking toughs, kept going for the watch.

Ralph grabbed the knife, grunted *"Motherfucker I'll kill you!"* and flashed the blade threateningly near the guy's neck, despite him still pulling and scratching at his wrist. A punch to the assailant's head from his right hand jostled them into each other, forcing the blade forward to cut the guys neck, spurting blood onto both of them.

Equally shocked, the attacker, who by now had finally broken the tiny springs that held the watchband in place, stumbled and grabbed his throat, but held on to that damn watch. That stupid $100 watch. Ralph, unrecognizably snorting and on fire with fury, kicked the man in his ribs with his knee as he was rising to run along with the other two men who had released Fotini from their grip.

Ralph quickly turned to Fotini, less one wristwatch but with the bloody knife still in his hand, and, wild-eyed and gasping, grabbed her and held her tight. *"Are you okay*?!"

"Yes, yes what happened?!" gasped Fotini. At that moment, though, almost impossible to be further incensed, seeing that Fotini was not hurt, he turned to run after the group. Three of guys had already gone too far down the street, but Ralph was after the red-head, ready to cut him to ribbons.

Ralph knew he was no Adonis – pudgy, bald (-ing), pale-skinned. He tried hard to shrug all that off whenever he was with Fotini – for himself and for every male smirk he saw coming at him as they walked together. But Ralph reached deep into his lifetime well of sadness, rejection and teasing and came out with hands as big as the Hulk.

He'd been truly enraged only once before in his life, that street hockey game a long time ago. This was very, very different. *Ralph was different.* Knowing he had gotten not only two punches in but had cut him, Ralph felt unstoppable and began to run after the guy. The watch was meaningless, but Ralph's pride and need to protect Fotini were like an IV of nitroglycerin.

He quickly looked down at his hand gripping the knife and realized how bloody it was but unthinkingly bolted off again, slipping at his first step from the blood on the *"panots"* in front of him.

He got about ten yards when his other senses kicked in and heard Fotini screaming, this time with fear "Ralph no! *No!* He was sure he could have caught the redhead but when he heard Fotini, he stopped and quickly returned to her.

"Are you okay? *Are you okay Fotini?"* Ralph nearly shouted, trembling and dizzy from the panic and his brutal response.

"Yes! Shit Ralph, look at your hand!"

"Are *you* okay? Tell me!"

"Yes they didn't hurt me. They just held me from helping you. Are you cut?"

"What?" Ralph's mind was in a frenzy, trying to process every moment of the last twenty-five seconds. He then looked down again at his bloody hand, furious, wild-eyed but gratefully realizing Fotini was not hurt. He wasn't sure if he was actually hurt but that didn't matter:

she was safe. He was so furious at that point he would neither have known nor cared if he was hurt.

Fotini was safe.

The group had all run off into the dark backstreets and alleyways, but one of them was trailing blood. They were both shocked at how much blood was on the *panots,* Ralph's shirt, pants and shoes.

Taking a deep breath, they turned and walked quickly toward Fotini's hotel but not before Ralph turned to see what and who might be behind him. Again. The lights of the barbershop were now off, the door locked.

At the hotel, they were met by Luigi, the nice young man at the door, who gasped at the sight of Ralph. "*Que pasa, que pasando, ostia, lo que te paso?*"

"Oh my god, there were guys hanging out around the corner and they attacked us!" Fotini exclaimed.

"*Hombre,* I will call the police for you?"

"No, no police, please" said Ralph. "Let's just go upstairs and let me get cleaned up."

"*Seguro?* Are you sure sir? This looks very bad sir!"

"Yes, no, no police, please."

Ralph wanted to get into Fotini's room, make no mistake, like he dreamed of getting into Maria Tremonti's room, but definitely not like this.

They stood silently in the elevator, still wound up, their minds replaying the attack, each second of it, in slow motion, second guessing everything.

Once inside her room, Fotini turned to go to the bathroom to get some towels, but Ralph grabbed her, spun her around, held her close and whispered "I'm glad, very glad, you are okay Fotini."

"Oh fuck Ralph, I'm so happy that *you* are okay, I think? You were very, *very* brave, Mr. Ralph."

She took Ralph's face in her hands and kissed him. Hard. Deeply. Without warning, but with the force of gratitude behind it.

"C'mon, we have to get you cleaned up."

No one had ever called Ralph brave before, not even Mrs. Neumann. No one ever had to, perhaps, but no one had ever even thought it, he was sure.

"I should have kicked those guys in the balls! Oh my god, how *crazy!*'" Fotini laughingly shrieked.

"Ha! A little action at Posidonia, eh?" Ralph bravely said, now even dizzier from Fotini's unexpected kiss. "But wow, that *was* crazy! All these years living in New York, supposedly so dangerous, and this *never* happened to me! I never even saw it happen to anyone else. Wow, just wow! But I am going to say it again, I am so grateful you are okay Fotini. It could have been a *lot* worse, for both of us."

"My God, what if *he* had a knife? Or those two guys? Really they didn't touch me except for holding my arms, but…Oh!" the gravity of it all hit Fotini and she quickly braced herself against the bathroom sink. Ralph's wrists and arms were deeply scratched but Ralph took great war-wound pride in knowing he tagged that little redheaded fucker back.

"Ralph, seriously, there was a lot of blood coming from that guy? Do you think he is okay?"

"I'm sure he is. It's just a small pen knife, only two inches long, but maybe it hit a good spot. I don't know but yes, I'm sure."

"I think I'm sure."

Drinks, nervous laughter, hugs and suddenly, warm kisses filled Fotini's room. Every single aspect of the past few days, had been unexpected. Dreamt of, yes. Hoped for, absolutely. But never really believed to be possible. The good or the bad.

Until then. The kiss that was nervous gratitude became passionate and the trembling, now excited affection. Finally, with their heart rates returning to normal, Ralph said "You better get some rest, Fotini. Tomorrow is your big presentation."

"Oh God Ralph how will I ever fall asleep?"

"Have another drink, maybe?" as they both laughed. "I should get back to my hotel and get these clothes off. Now, are you *sure* you're okay?"

"Yes, I'm sure, my brave Mr. Ralph. You are my hero!" More hugs and kisses followed and then Ralph was out the door. Once in the elevator, Ralph smiled to himself and repeated Fotini's words "… *my* brave Mr. Ralph…"

New message from Ralph: "Holy shit, man, do I have a story for *you*!"

Ralph told Luigi the story when he went downstairs but re-iterated his desire to not contact the police. He made sure to look both ways when he left and quickly but proudly slipped into his hotel, rushing past the front desk, at a kind of angle, so they might not see his bloody clothes.

Once safely in his room, he stood in front of the mirror and quietly nodded, whispering "Super Neumann…*Super Fucking Neumann*."

Lying in bed, trying to process *everything* that had just happened, Ralph exulted for a while and then shot up in a complete panic. Holy shit, he thought, What if there were cameras on the street? Fuck me, there are cameras everywhere these days!

His mind began playing devil-and-angel-on-each-shoulder, locked in a debate to the death:

Devil: No, no way, it's a tiny street! No way there are cameras! Stop worrying!

Angel: But he *did* bleed quite a bit – Damn it was only a two-inch blade, how much harm could that have caused? What if he went to the police? Or one of those other fuckers did?

Devil: No *wayyyy*, how could they have the balls to go to the police after trying to rob you?

Angel: But what if that guy died?

Devil: It was in self-defense! They have laws like that here, no? Fuck that guy, man!

Heart racing again, Ralph quickly threw on some pants and a long sleeve shirt to hide his bandages and ran out to check the street.

Nothing. Not a camera in sight. Not even any of those scumbags returning to the scene of the crime. A deep, exhausted and triumphant sleep quickly followed.

The Day After

"LADIES AND GENTLEMEN, IT IS OUR GREAT PLEASURE here at Posidonia to welcome one of the world's foremost experts on life and death in the oceans, Ms. Fotini Eleftheriou."

"Thank you. Thank you so much! I am truly honored to be here with you today, but before I begin my presentation, I have to tell you all I almost didn't make it here. This is my first time in Barcelona and it is an unquestionably beautiful city. But every city has its unpleasant side too and I was attacked on the street last night, a dark and clearly dangerous street. I am with you today because I was rescued by one of your colleagues here at Posidonia. Please, please let's all say thank you to Mr. Ralph Neumann of League Leader Cargo in New York, who was with me and bravely, valiantly, fought off the attackers! Ralph, would you please stand up?"

Murmurs of concern gave way to whistles and embarrassing applause as three thousand heads swiveled looking for this "Mr. Ralph" guy. The old Ralph would have sat in the back, in the shadows, but not today. Not the new Super Neumann. Ralph was in the third row and now in the very bullseye of attention. He gulped and stood, giving a short wave to the room and then blew a kiss to Fotini. He then just as quickly, sat down, red faced but incandescent with pride.

Fotini was seemingly none the worse for wear the next day: she was a dynamic and thoroughly engaging speaker and the topic, rising ocean temperatures and the effects on both land and sea, fully held the room's attention. She offered to meet anyone by the stage at the end of her speech for questions, but beyond making Ralph the "man-of-the-moment" with her public praise, he became the man-of-his-lifetime when she walked up to him, took his hand and placed him next to her as people thronged them both, with questions for her and handshakes for him. Ralph truly felt ten feet tall and wore his bandaged scratches like a war medal.

Ralph and Fotini met after the lunch break and ditched the rest of Posidonia for a long afternoon in the sun. Natalia, already one-for-one on her La Carassa recommendation, suggested a walk by the yachts and then along the boardwalk with a stop in the La Barceloneta neighborhood for a snack, and so they went.

Passeig de Joan de Borbo was a long stretch running parallel to the harbor, which was lined at length with restaurants on one side and yachts on the other. At the end, the path turned east and became a sensational boardwalk along the Mediterranean Sea, with colorful vendors of drinks and *pareos*, sand sculptures, bikers, skateboarders, joggers and couples strolling along. When they reached the end of the walk, in front of the giant bronze whale sculpture fronting the Hotel Arts tower, they did a U-turn and headed "into" the Barceloneta quarter.

The barrio was an intriguing grid of streets packed with low-rise apartment buildings, small bars and restaurants. "Bar Jai-Ca" was highly recommended by Queen Natalia and it was, again, an excellent choice. A small cold beer – una *cana* – and a few fried seafood dishes and they were off again, retracing their steps back towards...hmmm. Where? The hotel, perhaps? Fotini silently shared that curiosity.

Replaying the nights events over and over on their walk along the beach, complete with an additional and heartfelt hug or two from a still-grateful Fotini, Ralph boldly said "Well, that's that. Let's put it behind us and go forward, shall we?"

"Yes I agree Ralph." Silence followed as they both processed what "forward" might actually mean for them.

By this time, Ralph's phone had exploded with messages from Oscar, which made Ralph laugh out loud and smirk in a way he never had before, not to break Oscar's balls, but to finally have a story of his own to tell.

Above and below the surface, Ralph and Fotini were very much opposites, and yet, their life of aching solitude quietly but insistently tugged at them both. Fotini was accomplished; multilingual; smart on many levels and applications of her intelligence; genuinely, seductively attractive; and overall, well-balanced. Her apparent shyness was more of a qualitative judgement. She was surely social but also highly judicious with whom she spent her time and shared her intellect, and that gave her long periods of loneliness with few, at least in her small island world, who qualified for her attention.

Ralph was really none of what Fotini was: he was unaccomplished academically, professionally stale, knew a single language and had absorbed whatever minimal "culture" could be gleaned from living on Long Island. He wasn't hideous, but also not a head-turner of a man by any means.

He. Just. Was.

Fotini was always too much of everything for anyone to handle. Ralph was never enough of anything for anyone to be considered.

That loneliness had also quieted Ralph and his hopes, dreams and imagination further down into disappointed places that rarely saw light. But the moment Michael had told him about this trip, staring into that bathroom mirror at LLC, LLC after leaping for joy, Ralph dared himself to change his mindset, to go from wishful thinking to wish-fulfilled thinking.

For Fotini it was just another trip. Her expectations and preparations were all about her presentation, not to a man, but to her industry. Hope was not something Fotini, a woman of science, placed much value or belief in.

Life is often serendipitous, though for many, the moments between revelations are long and empty and painful. Each in their own way, this was the story for Ralph and Fotini, though they arrived at the same point, this point, from opposite directions: one filled with irrational hope, one dismissive of it.

Yet here they were, experiencing emotions and events, smells, tastes, images, sensations, fears and now, most definitely, even dreams. Together. They had kissed, not in moments of exploding passion, but in fearful gratitude. But they did kiss and it was neither unwelcome nor unpleasant. And both, after the fact, wanted more because both had so much less of it in their lives.

As they walked back toward their hotel (s) Ralph knew this was his moment. Fotini thought much the same yet both were silently unsure of how to proceed, exactly.

Opportunities such as this rarely came along for either one of them, by choice or by destiny. Fotini recognized this and suddenly suggested, in mid-sentence, they go back to her hotel for a drink.

"Let's get out of the sun for a bit and have a drink at my hotel. What do you say Ralph?

And so they did. Drinks in "Contraban," the cool, dark romantic lounge of the Hotel Wittmore fueled their what-shall-we-do-on-our-last-day discussion, a *vermut* for Ralph and a gin and tonic for Fotini in a giant, Spanish-style goblet of a glass. They sat and laughed and wondered and looked and sensed and tacitly dreamed: for the first time, they took off their mental blindfolds and smilingly, slyly undressed each other.

Drinks finished, Fotini, a bit flushed from the gin and from her own boldness, announced: "Ralph, let's have a siesta!" Instead of being red-faced or confused (even though he had no *real* idea of what she meant) (well a man can dream, can't he?) Ralph smiled wryly and went with it. "Great!"

Ralph had made it to Fotini's room on that fateful night, and allowed himself a quick peek of it. Small, a bit dark and naturally dominated by the bed, he tucked that image in his head, lest he never return. But now, he was on his way. He did not have to beg or to chase this. He was not rejected six times before the door opened. He didn't even have to pay for this: he was invited!

Fotini closed the curtains just enough to darken the room a bit more but allowing for two slivers of light to enter. "Come", she said, patting the bed. "Come here Mr. Ralph." The invitation to her bed actually was less compelling than the way she said "Mr. Ralph." In Ralph's head, he heard "C'mere big boy! C'mere my man!" They laid on the bed together, fully clothed, and talked quietly, about everything: the past three days. The night to come. Thursday. And most of all, "What happens next?" as they were both leaving on Friday. Less nervous than ever before, they allowed the other to wonder aloud.

"Look, I know we said, let's put the other night behind us. But Ralph, I can't stop thinking about that boy and the blood on the *panots*."

"Truthfully, neither can I. It's ironic that my little knife could cause so much blood, but really, what could have happened? I did *not* directly stab him. I just put the blade to his neck to threaten him but when I punched him, our bodies pushed against each other and the blade was there. Still, yes, I saw the blood, for sure, but…Well, maybe it wasn't so much? The sight of blood is more shocking than the actual amount, don't you think?"

Neither had an answer for Friday, but both knew, as they sweetly and increasingly entangled themselves, that they did not want things to end on Friday.

The devil and angel popped up on each of Ralph's shoulders again:

Devil: Seize the moment – Dude, *you are in her bed!*

Angel: Idiot, you are at the finish line – don't be clumsy and trip just before it!

Devil: Did you hear how she said "C'mere Mr. Ralph?" She wants you! Be a fucking man and take charge!"

Favorite porn scenarios danced in Ralph's head and tugged at his belt, but he just went with the flow. Despite her bold invitation, Fotini fought every urge she'd had in the last five years to seize her own moment, not wanting her father to be upset with her by charging to the front, or on top, or any other position.

Stalemate. But for just a few more moments.

Ralph could no longer comfortably hide his literal excitement and Fotini could no longer ignore it.

And so it began.

Fotini was taut, sexy, athletic, intense fun and for once, for Ralph, real and not a computer screen. Ralph was a warm bear of a man for her, tender but forceful, and performed like a champion. They both pushed past their own hesitancies and fears (and for Ralph, weird fetishes) and left each other in a stunned, crumpled, gasping, delighted mess. The veil had been lifted, their protective skin pierced and this strange trip they had been on since 8:45 am Monday morning, through placid blue waters and roiling, violent rogue waves battering them, now charted a new course to an unknown destination. A path lay ahead for them to travel with and towards each other.

"Ralph, I think you might love Cyprus! Our beaches are small but some of them are like postcards – They *are* postcards! And to sit in a tiny café in the countryside, listing to bells of the goats in the fields, eating fabulous *souvla* from the grill, well, it's quite beautiful."

"Let's go swimming in the ocean of dreams…it's off the coast of "desire". The water there is always warm and clear."

"Hmm it does sound much nicer than where I live. But Jones Beach is great, does that count? We can count my clients ships on the horizon! Did you ever visit the Hamptons when you came to New York"?"

"It all counts, Ralph. I have not been back to New York in many years – Maybe we should think about this?"

"Really? Well, can I tell you a little secret? I already have."

Blushing deeply, Fotini just smiled, sparkled and then kissed him deeply, within an inch of his consciousness.

Dinner that night was a special multi-course tasting menu feast at Fonda Espana, followed by a viewing of the "magic fountain" show at the Plaza Espana and a snuggled taxi ride back to Ralph's hotel. Fotini even urged Ralph to put his seatbelt on in the cab, to protect him. Ralph had once made a kind of mixtape for himself of what he thought were mellow, romantic, candle lit songs and then sat in his big easy chair at home, alone, and mostly moped. But now? No chair, no moping: Ralph and Fotini slow danced body-to-body, wrapped so tightly you could not tell where Ralph began and Fotini ended. They swayed together for hours and that playlist would now be a march of triumph and no longer a funeral dirge.

They made Thursday "Barcelona culture day:" visits to the famous (and awe-inspiring) Gaudi sites of the Sagrada Familia church, Park Guell, Casa Battlo and finally the rooftop of La Pedrera, where they held hands and kissed in a very special, forever-to-be-remembered way.

Dinner was at a lovely restaurant that seemed almost like a private home, "Raco d'en Cesc". Over delicious and exotic Catalan cuisine they agreed it was time to talk about Friday and beyond.

"Please Ralph, let's not call this a 'farewell dinner'?"

"No, Fotini, its, I hope, I think, just the opposite. You have no idea how much I want to do this, to go with you! You've made Cyprus sound fabulous and I wish, I so wish I could go home with you, even for just the weekend, but I do have to go back to New York tomorrow and prepare my report for work on Monday."

"Ralph, listen to me: we are both almost forty years old now. These past few days have opened my eyes to so many things for me, so many "first" things: meeting you by accident, this city, the food we've tried, the things we have experienced, your sweet and brave kindness and oh, yes your manly sexiness, too! I know it's a cliché but we could be gone tomorrow – What if one of those guys had a knife or even a gun? I mean, I know it's not New York with all your guns but it's really given me a totally new outlook on my life and if you can't come back to Cyprus with me, maybe I could come to New York with you? I'm just not ready or prepared to say"… goodbye, see you soon, let's stay in touch…"

Ralph was flabbergasted but equally so, utterly entranced. The notion to impetuously run off with this incredible woman and literally leave the "old" Ralph behind made him dizzy, and tempted! Now, she was suggesting to come to New York? With *him*? What the what?

"Time is passing Ralph. I work independently, I have no office to return to. I am a free woman. Please, I'm sorry, am I being too much now?"

"No, *no*! I mean, just, wow, I'd have a million things to consider, but…but, yes let's consider them!" Images of his speechless mother, along with the idea of bringing Fotini to the office and showing her off like a trophy to all those arrogant, stupid vest-wearing douche bags in the Sales department made him both cringe and laugh out loud.

"Allow me to state the obvious, Fotini: you are a genuinely beautiful woman and I am, well, not a movie star or a Greek god."

"Believe me Ralph, my life has always been one of substance over surface. You have shown me so much of the man you are."

Ralph had feared that night would be a "midnight for Cinderella" story, that it would all go poof! and he would turn back into a pumpkin. At first, he thought he could live with it: the never-ending replay in his head of every incredible moment would have to carry him forward. But Fotini's boldness Wednesday night and her "we-are-nearly-forty-now" declarations also made him think hard. I will surely *never* get a chance with a woman like this again, he thought. His life, which had dragged painfully slowly before Fotini, had now completely shifted off its axis of predictability and he began to panic, questioning whether he could be happy with an amazing story and…then go back to being "Ralphie boooyy" again. Alone. Sitting in the dark in his easy chair with a bag of chips, listening to the music they had danced and fucked to like rabbits.

Days come and days go, and evenings follow suit, but when it's all said and done, who will be there to sit with you, in the quiet moments, as the light fades down the walls of your room?

For Ralph, this was not a "full circle" moment. He did not live a rollercoaster life, but a very linear, straight-line path to routine normality. But now everything, *everything* had changed and for once, and *finally*, for the better.

Ralph came to Posidonia thinking he would go drinking with Filipino guys. Maybe he'd even pay for an hour with a nice Spanish girl. Instead, he fucked an amazing Greek woman and bloodied a Spanish boy. Not even Oscar would believe what he barely believed himself.

For Fotini, it was a moment of "What if you find everything you ever wanted when you weren't looking for it?"

"What about your plane ticket?" Ralph asked.

"Don't worry, it was cheap and I have a friend at Olympic who will arrange a credit. I am sure they can get me on your flight."

"How about clothes? Do you have enough cl...?"

Fotini leaned in and kissed Ralph long and deeply. "Yes, Ralph I have whatever I need."

Adios Barcelona

DELTA AIRLINES FLIGHT # 169 left Barcelona at 2.00 for New York but Ralph wanted to, again, get to the airport plenty early to enjoy the private club amenities in the Salon VIP Joan Miro at Barcelona's El Prat airport. Okay, maybe he'd spend a bit more time checking out Barcelona's duty free, for one last gift, but that whole private lounge thing, now with the beautiful Fotini literally in hand, seemed much more pleasurable and he loved playing big shot and showing her he can get into VIP places.

They were third in line to check in and focused solely on each other, never noticing the small cluster of police idly chatting off to the side. When they stepped forward to the Delta desk agent and handed over their passports, Ralph noticed her expression change and flush just a bit. Weird, he thought, and then thought nothing more of it while he turned to help Fotini put her suitcase on the scale.

Suddenly, four officers in various uniforms were beside them. One of them spoke English and confirmed it was Ralph. Now Ralph was the one who flushed red and looked scared.

"Ralph Neumann? You live in New York? Please come with us." "Wait, what is this? What's going on?" Equal parts petrified, confused and embarrassed in front of Fotini, this just had to be a terrible joke, right? But no one, not even Oscar or Michael, would do this to him.

"Hey, wait!" shouted Fotini, as she was led off to the side of the check-in desk by a female officer. "What is happening here?"

"Please, Miss, please, with me, please" said the agent as she stared over her shoulder to see Ralph being put into handcuffs.

"Wait a second!" Ralph now shouted. "Explain to me what the hell is going on!"

"Fotini! Fotini wait for me!"

"Ralph! I love you Ralph! Don't say anything! Don't say anything!"

New message from Ralph: Please let Michael know I might be late for work on Monday.

League Leader Cargo was sleepy and quiet Monday morning. As folks shuffled in with their coffees and bagels, most paid no mind to the two police cars parked in front of the building. But when they entered the office, the sight of not only two uniformed officers but three men in suits and badges definitely got their attention. The group chatter exploded.

"What the fuck is going on?"

"Did a ship with drugs sink?"

"Uh, oh, who has been sexually harassing who?"

Tina ran interference for Michael, shooing people away, but when the word got around that it involved Ralph, eyes bulged and heads shook in complete incredulity. *"Who?"* *"Ralph?!?* Ralphie boooyy? It's not possible!"

When Oscar emerged from the conference room, shaking, a bit pale and with a weak smile, the emails began to fly. Michael thanked the officers and then called a company-wide meeting in the center of the room.

"All cellphones off please, right now" he announced. "Well, it seems our Ralphie boooyy got himself into a bit of a scrape at Posidonia! Turns out, he was mugged, *but managed to fight off the gang of attackers!* In doing so, and let me add another layer of amazement to this story, he was not only protecting himself, *but the woman he was with, too!"*

Heads were held in hands, smiles beamed, mouths were covered in shock and a few folks flat out laughed. Stunned amazement made its way around the room.

"It seems Ralph popped this guy really good, somehow cutting his throat in the process. Incredibly, when the guy went to the hospital, he claimed Ralph attacked *him!"*

Cries of *"whaaaaat*? Holy Shit! *Ralph???* Our Ralphie boooyy?"

"Ralph is currently being held in Barcelona so the police are here gathering evidence and checking information. Oscar confirmed Ralph's story."

"Our Ralphie boooyy is a hero!"

"But, but Oscar, how do you know all this?" asked a stunned Felipe from the Cargo Insurance division.

"Because Ralph and I are good friends, and we have been texting ever since he left the office last week. He told me everything and I just confirmed it all with the police. If all goes well, he will be here tomorrow – *with his new girlfriend!*" Jaws dropped and time seemed to stop all around the room.

"Okay folks, party's over. Back to work!" shouted Michael. "But let me say this: maybe, just maybe, this means he's not 'Ralphie boooyy' anymore but just plain Ralph? Everybody good with that?'"

They all had a good laugh, but this time, they were happy *for* Ralph and not laughing *at* him.

Super Neumann was coming home.

Freshman Infatuation

WHEN JONI MITCHELL FELL ILL, a radio station he was listening to played two songs on their "Two-fer Tuesday" segment from her album "Hejira". Hearing just the first three notes from Jaco Pastorius' bass line of "Coyote" made him grip the wheel and take a short, sharp breath in recollection of his first true love.

It was the fall of 1976. He was a freshman and didn't know better. She was a senior and should have.

Life is often serendipitous and beyond our measured control: a left turn instead of a right to miss the out-of-control taxi crashing on to the sidewalk; a missed flight and a seatmate that becomes your spouse on the next one; a second drink instead of calling it a night and all the hijinks that ensue.

Math 101 should have been a class filled with, um, freshmen but this was no freshman. She sat down next to him on day one in the only seat left in the room and offered a simple, eye-fluttering smile of seat-proximity recognition that he was sure whispered "Hello handsome boy".

He silently gulped and dropped both his pen and his notebook, as well as his flustered gaze, to the floor. Up until now, he was historically terrible in math. *He hated math.* But right then, he was digging math like never before.

Shy smiles and the flirtatious doodle-in-the-others-notebook followed three times per week, along with silent anguish when she was late (or when she simply blew off the class, as was her senior prerogative) and hence, seats together could not be had. But when they were side by side, they began to share something, something an eighteen year old had not felt before, and it was more than just the little Jolly Rancher watermelon candies he would secretly slip her when the teachers back was turned.

"...No regrets coyote we just come from such different sets of circumstance I'm up all night in the studios and you're up early on your ranch..."

She was the queen of the campus: a DJ on the college radio station, as beautiful as Sheryl Crow, as soulful as Bonnie Raitt and as tough as Chrissie Hynde. She drove an orange Fiat convertible. She was sexy and beautiful and a senior with a couple of odd math credits to make up. He was a scraggly, starry-eyed, besotted eighteen year old, beginning to understand for the very first time the soul-scorched welding of love and suffering. When not in class, he looked everywhere for her, not to talk necessarily, but just to see her, to nod nonchalantly when he did despite the fireworks exploding inside of him. Just a peek, just a taste was enough, he thought. Until it passed, and then he was hungry again.

All along their shared journey, they kept rising and falling for each other: the deep, growing affection; the feigned-but-heartbreaking indifference they showed when they saw the other speaking to someone of the opposite sex in a hallway; the dismissive derision of the freshman and his hangdog look when she sat with her senior friends in the cafeteria and paid him no mind. She tortured him, but she also loved him and she knew, she *must* have known, how he suffered. He spent literally hours sitting at his desk in front of the big picture window "studying" while listening to "Hejira" over and over, all for just seven seconds of seeing her car drive by on her way out of campus to her apartment. Listening to that album squeezed the blood out of his heart and left him pale and faint. Love, he feared, might not be for him, even though he was sure *she* was. The push-pull of it all left him dizzy and his GPA in the dust.

"...There's no comprehending just how close to the bone and the skin and the eyes and the lips you can get and still feel so alone..."

They propped each other up in math class and soon they laid down beside each other. All the stars aligned for one long, brilliant, life-changing late-afternoon-into-night-into-the-next-day for them. They shared watermelon candies to a scratchy soundtrack of Joni Mitchell and the Doobie Brothers and tried not to spill a can of grape soda between their bodies, a drink that seemed to ferment into sweet wine with each sip. They licked each other's tears at sunrise knowing both of their lives had changed forever over the last seventeen hours. Time, graduation and a four-year age difference separated them, though only physically. After many internet search's, he finally found her again on Facebook.

They admitted that they often, so often, had thought of one another and those days as the years passed, through husbands and wives and kids and dogs and mortgages and sickness and health. They admitted to still being starry eyed and would occasionally tragically mourn the boy and girl they both were then. She confessed to long recalling his liquid cocoa eyes and how a grape soda or watermelon candy always reduced her to silent smiles. He confessed to quietly buckling under the sensory weight every time he heard "Coyote".

Time had shown them both that true love knew no bounds of time, pleasure or pain. You can only have one, just one, first love, and for him, it was her.

The Ten Commandments

THE TEN COMMANDMENTS, REGARDLESS OF your personal religious P-O-V, exist and really, they are not *all* that ancient or outdated. I mean, *someone* would have jotted down these rights-and-wrongs, be it Nostradamus or a laughing Beelzebub, Shakespeare or St. Someone.

So we deal with them, usually dripping with guilty admonishment after breaking one of them, occasionally to smithereens.

"Don't kill." Fine, fair enough and pretty straightforward, don't you think?

"Don't gouge an eye for another's eye." Okay, that's not one of the commandments, but I think it very well could be a good amendment, after the fact. There *are* other ways to settle ones differences.

"Don't steal". And really, why should you steal anything, unless it's totally justified. Like money from the US Treasury.

"Don't covet thy neighbor's wife". In my town, that one's pretty easy to obey: all the women are bright and handsome and wear natural fibers and make Kraft Macaroni & Cheese for their kid's dinner and drive Acura's. Not much to incite my desire there.

But don't covet anything? By now, your neighbor's donkey, I think, has been replaced by your neighbors Land Rover and in the suburbs, it's pretty tough not to covet. We covet each other's snow blowers and vacations and for our teenagers, the SAT scores of our neighbor's kid.

However, "covet" and "wish" *are* different, no? I wish, deeply and without a single pang of guilt, to win the Powerball. I wish it would not snow one more single flake this winter. I wish the "check engine" light in my car would go out as quickly and mysteriously as it went on. I wish the 8.02 am Metro-North train would arrive at 8.03 am every single day, giving me those extra seconds to get down the stairs, with a golden seat reserved just for me, to end the indignity of standing on the Metro North once and for all.

People like to say "don't wish for money, you'll never get it or have enough". "Don't wish for love, you'll die alone". "Don't wish for health, you'll always be sick". The same people often say "Be careful what you wish for". You know why? Because they never got anything; because they never thought they would.

Or believed they could.

An Inconsolable Grief

BARCELONA, TO BE SURE, IS A CHARMING delight of a city. But like any city of millions, not everyone is living the good life. I'd seen her before. A few times. Mostly during the day and once at night, she was unmistakable on the streets.

Always bedraggled, always walking somewhere with a sense of purpose but, you could tell, never actually having a destination. But she was also not, seemingly, either homeless or aimless. The grief she bore wore her face into a spin-art of dirty lines and tear-streaked cheeks. A faded scarf around her neck. A stained shawl that dragged her shoulders down even further than her despair. A limp. Her coat was dirty, greasy, often wet from last nights' rain. The hem of her pants were filthy as they dragged along the ground over her scuffed sneakers, which were also nearly black and worn through at the toe.

I live on a street that, in effect, is a small village inside a big city. I suppose you could say that about any "neighborhood" anywhere and hence, regardless of your location you "run into" the same people or see them around, both friend and foe. You make judgments, you hear gossip, you see their movements and the movements of others literally sidestepping around them as they approach.

Like many of the bedraggled, either pushing a battered shopping cart or pulling tattered bags that hold all their worldly possessions, she was the bag type. Her hands were absolutely raw, red and blistered from carrying them through all the seasons, adding to her endless misery.

Oddly, inside one bag and among whatever she felt she could not part with and had to keep close by her side, there was always something "clinking" that you could hear with each shuffled step. Not coins-clink, but…glass? Ceramic pieces of something? Figurines? Each step brought a clink and a clatter.

I've seen a few shady characters on the block: the ragged guy with the dreadlocks always in a rush somewhere. The scrap-yard-ers, pushing their jerry-rigged bicycles attached to a cart filled with anyone's definition of scrap metal. The Pakistani fruit sellers moving boxes of apples and tomatoes from one cousin's shop to the other's. The propane gas man, clanking his spoon against the barrels, calling out to the street for a tank exchange from the very old apartments without a gas line.

In turn, each shopkeeper has their place in the daily rhythm of the street: the small *supermercado* owner who looks at his phone twelve hours a day, watching silly videos in-between sales of milk, cigarettes, candy and beer. He sees all, despite his head being down. The hall porter of one of the bigger buildings, a virtual Stasi agent for the block, keeping quiet tabs on who is coming or going. The tattoo parlor gang, hanging out and smoking up a storm, saying hi and waiting for their next human work of art. Each has their finger on the pulse of the street. And each "knew" the sad lady with the clinking shopping bags.

One day, I came to know her too. While walking down the dark, narrow Carrer de la Mare de Deu del Pilar, I saw her up ahead – that unmistakable limp, the faint-but-getting closer click-clack of her bag of tricks. She did not notice me. I suppose she really didn't notice anyone: since so many tried not to notice her, the effect was mutual. But as she passed me, she suddenly looked me in the eye, for barely two seconds, with a grief-stricken sadness that felt like a punch in the chest. I grimaced and barely pushed out a "reply" in my return of her glance somewhere between sadness, pity and pure empathy. My throat closed, turning my hard swallow at this exchange into a cough.

She continued down the street, but that moment, that single passing moment, really struck me hard, and I turned to watch her go. Why? I wasn't sure. At all. I didn't expect to see anything really.

But then I did. I saw the reason for her sadness, the near-destruction of her life, it seemed. She reached into the bag and pulled out a little yellow piece of…something, and placed it on top of a telephone box that was covered with stickers and a bit of graffiti, as they all are. And then continued on, shuffling along, click-clacking, her "package" delivered.

But a few steps later, she turned back towards me. Maybe she knew I was watching her. Maybe she *wanted* me to watch her, given our two seconds of humanity and acknowledgment. Maybe. I don't honestly know. But having "seen" her, eye to eye, she then felt it was okay for me to see her action, of that I am sure. We both saw something in that nervous passing glance.

People make a quick judgement when they stop you on the street – kind and trusting? Knowledgeable? Safe to approach? Dressed in their imagination as a local? I don't know what she saw, but all I saw was a soul pulverized by sadness and a need for some kind of help.

She did not beg. She did not hold out a dirty cup, or prostrate herself on the sidewalk, her face inches from the concrete, her hands raised in prayer and beseechment, like others all along the fashionable Passeig de Gracia.

I quickly stopped to "look" at my phone, head down, counting the seconds until I thought, logically, she would have continued on. I prayed that when I looked up, she would not still be there, looking back at me. I pointlessly peeked in a shop window, buying another five seconds, until I "acted" like maybe I forgot something, turned to re-trace the steps of the street but really to peek and make sure she had gone.

Coast clear, I went back to the phone box to see what it was, what clue this woman had hidden in plain sight for me and everyone who ever avoided her glance to see. Hesitant to touch it, I was compelled nonetheless, making sure to return it to the exact spot where she'd left it. I was fascinated, and yet a bit repulsed by my own curiosity.

It was a little Lego piece. Three yellow stacked bricks. At the bottom of it was a tiny piece of paper with a mobile phone number written on it, barely attached with dirty, curling tape. I gulped, head spinning, and quickly replaced it down to the centimeter of its position, gave a fast glance up the street again to see if I had been "caught" and double-timed it in the opposite direction, flat-out scared, shaking and dizzy.

The human heart can break for many reasons, some true and honest, some contrived to gather sympathy or more likes on your Instagram page. My chest felt bruised if not crushed.

The haunting of the entire event, those few seconds, really left me rattled. I asked the block spies, my bodega guy and the sexy tattoo artist across the street what the story was, to know, to understand, and to confirm both my suspicions and fears.

It seems this woman's son had been kidnapped some time ago. Left alone outside a friendly neighborhood shop for the same few seconds it took for her and I to look at each other, her little boy was gone, and now she searched, desperately, everywhere, with the "bread-crumbs" of his favorite Lego's to guide him back to her. Barcelona is not yet a city saturated with video cameras on every light pole, and definitely not in the old part of town, with its narrow, shaded ancient streets

The eternal bond of a mother and her only son is simply unbreakable and she held tight to the conviction that someday they would find each other again.

The hope and help of others had long since faded into helpless pity, but she does not quit; clearly she will not quit. She cannot quit. What else are a mother and son to do when they are both lost and looking for each other?

(WHI)NEwyork

(with deepest respect to Alan Ginsburg)

I SAW THE BEST YOUNG MINDS of this generation destroyed by Bitcoin and ramen, humbled by Bumble and scorched by their Tinder tenders of love

Whose curated Instagram dreams of Coachella weekends and another round of twenty-two dollar ("debit-or-credit?") cocktails with straight-from-a melting-glacier ice cubes and sick Scoville-rating sustainable chili swizzle sticks spin the polar vortex counterclockwise toward next quarter's earnings report

Whose revolution was not televised, but streamed on the device of their choice

Whose data plan are the shackles of their aspirational slavery by the minds of the oppressor Godhead FAANG

Whose Citibike forays down gentrified avenues and brownstone-studded EPA Superfund sites were set alight by angry now-where-do-we-go neighborhoods all but re-developed into shiny unrecognizability

Whose frat house dreams and wan, cellphones-still-paid-for-by-their parents smilegrimace at the Whole Foods checkout signal to the other knit caps the utter sadness of their kale-and-quinoa bowl sustenance

Whose finger-licking swiping tothelefttotherighttotheleft is the friction spark to keep the fires of their comparative loneliness from frostbite in the bombogenesis of their doorman building

I saw them abandon the L train and flock, huddled and shivering in gaggles of Canada Goose, their Yeezyfeet swaddled in Rag & Bone

I saw them line up for tacos and soup dumplings in the furnace that is Flushing in August and the shimmering Siberia that is Bushwick in December, shuffling their Allbirds while dreaming of Uber Eats nights choking on the vape fumes of Netflix-charred cuddles on their Housing Works couches

I am with you at Santa Con, white beards matted with brown, malty/hoppy/citrusy/caramel-y grapefruit-infused vomited wort!

I am with you at Occupy Wall Street and Black Lives Matter, blowing a whistle at the inherent privilege of whiteness and banging a tin can in my authentic fiber-wicking antifa yoga pants that is dinner from the deposit for the homeless person you think you are saving

I am with you at happy hour, drowning my data-optimized day in a Red Bull-and-anything-the-bartender-suggests, an alcoholic omakase

Pride month

flat earth

pro-life

anti-vaxxcovidcovidcovidcovidcovidcovidcovidcovidcovidcovid

pitch clock

book bans

drone strikes

rigged elections

tik-tok-ya-don't-stop

influencers and refugees

debt ceiling wildfires and secret documents

woke yet ignorant

rivers of gender fluidity irrigating confusion to bloom

And to it all, I say "Liberty Liberty Liberty....Liberty"

A Future Time

HAVE YOU IMAGINED HOW YOU WILL DIE? More so, have you (and really now, who hasn't?) imagined how you would *like* to die? Or are you of the stupid-sticous ilk that says "Hush!" or "God forbid, don't talk like that!" as if the discussion itself will somehow get you in the neck, perhaps the very next day; as if *not* talking about it can actually stave off your ultimate demise.

I went a long way in my life, many, many years, without the death of anyone within my arm's reach. Two grandparent's years ago and years apart, but that was pretty much it. It was a good long run, but now naturally I am giving back all my winnings to the house: parents, relatives, husbands and wives of close friends, and close friends themselves.

Life is a gamble every day, isn't it? We roll the dice every time we start the car, every time we cross the street and miss the falling piano.

To be honest, I was never really comfortable with the whole wake-followed-by-"memorial meal" thing. The idea of sandwiches and drinks after digging a hole in the ground for a close friend has always been just plain bizarre to me. But I understood it after my mother died. It really did feel good to see friends, hug friends and even laugh with a friend at that moment. And I surprised myself by not feeling like I had cheated my mother out of the necessary grief quotient. I grieved plenty and I miss her still, every single day.

So, have you? Have you peeked into a future time to see your own death? My mother died at eighty-four, my father at ninety-four – not bad numbers as these things go. Neither had a day of pain. They died in their own home. So really, what more could I ask of God?

Well, maybe, just this: to die as I hope to. To be old, but not so old as to have a Jamaican nurse and be forced to wear stained sweatpants and Velcro shuffle-along shoes.

To be healthy, and not have my days filled with hospital ceilings as my only view and bedpan effluent as my only companion in bed while my feeble mind clings to something long past. To be happy, or as happy as I can be when I look back on it all.

I want to die on a sunny summer afternoon on a hammock strung between two cypress trees on the grounds of my stone farmhouse which is on a rise overlooking the Mediterranean. And while I'm asking, make it at about 5:30 on a warm, summer afternoon, if you please, God?

I'd like a belly full of grilled fish and two glasses of wine along with a still-lit but fading cigar between my fingers resting on my chest.

I truly hope this is where they will find me when my sweet grandkids run to get one of my sons and says "Grandpa is sleeping and won't get up to play with us."

One Flight Down

Bon dia!

EVERY DAY BEGINS THE SAME way for most of us, for so many of us: alarm clock>>toothbrush>>shower>>what to wear>>check the clock again. Do I have time for a coffee? Something to eat? Grab a bag>>grab a coat>>what is the temperature today?>>grab the keys – where *are* those damn keys?>>grab the phone>>grab the door and out we go, focused on the day ahead, and not the steps directly ahead. Same way, "same day" for pretty much everyone.

Down the hall>>wait for an elevator>>wait for a bus>>wait for a train>>wait for your coffee and croissant>>wait for the light>>wait for the slow poke ahead of you>>wait for the revolving door>>wait for the elevator (again) and finally, arrive, at your desk>>your school>>the awful shared countertop where you work.

For Toni, Monday began no differently than any other Monday or any other workday, for that matter. Pattern executed as per.

With head down, one sleeve still swinging free while trying to find the little pocket for the house keys and of course, balancing the phone and backpack, Toni stepped unknowingly toward what seemed to be another day. But on this day, steps became leaps from every other day and toward altogether new and better days ahead.

The go-getter in him barreled out the door and then proceeded to crash (politely) into apartment 1, across the hall from his, apartment. 2. It was a near-fatal, highway-like incident, without the broken glass, the blown tires or leaking radiator fluid, but with the trauma of the shock of the bump, unseen before the collision.

"*Ostia! Lo siento mucho!* I'm *so* sorry!" Toni exclaimed as he bent down to pick up his keys and her phone, thrown like passengers without seatbelts. The neck-snapping collision actually happened seconds later, when bent, flushed and scrambling, he saw the well-turned ankle, the colorful and fashionable heels, and the fringe of the hem of her jeans as he rose and caught his breath.

"*Ay dios, mio*, I'm so sorry, I'm a bit late for work" a flustered Toni stammered again, this time in English.

"*Joder*! I mean, Sorry, so am I. Yes, yes, are *you* ok?" searched Paloma, now eye to eye with apartment. 2. (*Hell yes*, he thought!!) Red-faced from the collision and flushed with the instant recognition of beguiling eyes and a warm, no-problem-at-all-smile, Paloma felt herself in a state of utter and immediate confusion, not from the bump, but from the bump-er.

"Yes, yes, are you *sure* YOU are ok?" searched Toni, (Toni knew she was OK, but wanted another moment of "concern and tender caring" to implant itself) now eye to eye with apartment 1, red-faced from the collision and flushed with the instant recognition of beguiling eyes and a warm, no-problem-at-all-smile. He was new to the building at 11, Carrrer de l'Argenteria, the one with the fancy scrollwork on the front door. Bon dia indeed!

Toni's weekend had been spent spending and running, here and there, to fill in the blank spaces of his new apartment: knick-knacks and kitchen utensils, bathroom stuff, a throw rug, a small lamp, new sheets and towels that he wanted fresh for himself. The rest of the furnished apartment were necessities that he'd have to get over their previously-used state, but all was well. He didn't require all that much, but what he did had to be good if only for his self-image and not for the expectedly-rare visitors.

That, however, might have just changed.

He was, in equal measure, embarrassed and instantly besotted. He stammered and gulped (and panicked, just a bit) and distractedly said "Oh, grrr I forgot something inside. Sorry again! Have a nice day!" and quickly slipped back inside his apartment, shut the door and spun around, resting against it and trying to make himself so thin he could pass through it while still closed. Chest thumping wildly, he counted to one hundred, figuring that was enough time for her to go down and out the door without another mid-air collision as well as allow his red face to return to normal. But he nonetheless peeked through the keyhole like Mr. Bean, searching wildly, just in case.

Over the first quick coffee of the day, he half-knew/half-feared that both his clumsiness and hypnosis had blinked LED-bright in front of her. The day then attempted to get back on its track, but he was wobbly all morning – that flash, that moment of impact was not just about the physics of one body in motion striking another, but something else he could not shake. It would not fall harmlessly and pointlessly into the garbage can of daily events. Was there an equal and opposite reaction? He obsessed all morning. His head was as focused as an overdose of Benadryl.

Toni was starting a new job and new Chapter in his life, teaching English. Single, free, hungry for adventure and sick of New York after being unfairly downsized, he hit upon this idea and with more luck than research or planning, landed this new gig.

Unbeknownst to him, the prologue and epilogue were waiting for him, one across the hall, the other one flight up. Toni did not know it yet, but he just met Paloma, an angel in search of chaos. He was also soon to meet Carmen, a demon in search of peace.

Paloma

Every woman wants a man where she can climb on his lap, where she finds peace. Resting her head on his shoulder, without words or sudden movements. Just sit and listen to his strong and warm heartbeat, to feel protected and to know that his heart is only beating for her. Every woman needs the hands that are ready to catch her, that will never let her go.

(ANONYMOUS INTERNET PHILOSOPHER)

PALOMA HAD LIVED IN THE BUILDING for a few years. She liked her place. She liked her barrio, the shops and the shopkeepers and the vibe of the neighborhood. Mostly.

But that's all it was: "like". Fine.

Like her life.

Paloma was *very* attractive, by anyone's definition and standards. And she knew it, but she also had a hidden hard edge. Yes, to be sure, she was fun, agreeable, friendly, a good colleague, nice neighbor to La Senora and generally...happy. Well, at least you could say "content", which by its definition expresses a *lack* of happiness.

She was smart and very often too smart for everyone else's good. She loved food and wine and sensual pleasures as such, but they were stand-ins for other inexplicably missing joys in her life. She had friends but none struck a particularly high note inside of her, though they didn't know that. She was fun to travel with, was considered very stylish, never exercised but was always in slender, impeccable shape and turned more than a few heads, male and female, intentionally and unintentionally.

Paloma went her own way, on her own terms, quietly, respectfully but definitively and pretty much did not care what others thought of her or her decisions.

She also doted on her father Nacho, who returned the love and adoration every minute of every day. She was very busy, rising at work at a top law firm, but still made time, above almost all else, to regularly check in on him and his caregiver, Marta, who was a Filipina angel to him. Paloma's mother had died suddenly ten years earlier, which made her relationship with Nacho even deeper than the typical father-daughter connection

But Paloma, living a good and seemingly very nice and carefree life, was also unloved. Her bed was empty and so was her heart. Coffee dates, lunch dates, dinner dates and even a boyfriend of sorts came and went, though no one or nothing as serious as Hector once was, a name she hated but a man she loved. Or so she thought. So life went on: happy, but meaningless. The pain of her solitude, especially the inexplicability of it, given her obvious beauty, made her cry privately as often as she smiled. She just could not lower her standards and was tormented by that fact, yet she knew any attempt to do so would be a greater disaster than if she had just held her ground and waited for her prince to come. But it hurt so much.

Unbeknownst to her, Toni had moved in earlier that week with life possessions that could not fill 3 suitcases during a day for her that had stretched long into the Barcelona evening of work, meetings, a deadline, a Zoom chat and a performance review that left her needing more than the usual after-work drink and *tapas*.

Though sight unseen, she had "heard" him and casually thought "Oh, someone must have finally moved into La Senora's apartment." Poor old woman, Paloma thought, too bad about her. No one wants to feel dependent on others, even family, but she had clearly become too frail to take care of herself. Paloma never minded buying a few things for her when she went shopping and she was always so gracious in her thanks to Paloma, inviting her for some tea and a cookie. God knows how old those cookies were.

Apartment 1 and apartment 2 at 11, Carrer de l'Argenteria shared a balcony that overlooked the neighbor's garden and a court-yard of backyards of various buildings. It allowed her to listen to his musical choices via the open terrace shutters as well as experience the "whispers to heaven" of his end-of-the-day cigar smoke, a bit of which managed to slip inside her window. She rather liked the smoke – it reminded her of her father. As for music, his tastes were diverse, from jazz, house, chill and the offbeat "worldbeat": rai, Afro-pop, Latin rhythms and odd, un-syncopated measures; music of the dusty world, usually made by people who find great happiness in what others may consider to be very small pleasures.

The Friday night playlist, which she only half-heard, exhausted as she was, was bouncy…stirring…sexy. Very Friday night, Paloma thought: Paloma was still young enough to think of Friday nights as "…a night with personality…"

"Once in a Lifetime" by Angelique Kidjo

"DJ's Gotta Dance More" by A-Trak

Music was a very important element of Toni's life – it helped him dream when quietly listening to it, even if the beat was raucous and furious. It took his mind places where he'd normally dare not go and reminded him of places he had dared to. He'd been a DJ on his small college radio station many years earlier and he often got good reviews and backslaps for his show when he returned to the dorm. He had very eclectic tastes in music (all except country music!) and he felt it represented a side of him well, the diversity of his thoughts, the slightly "cool mystery" of his persona, the images the music created in his head and the sensations in his soul. He loved to sit in the dark with headphones on to listen, immersed entirely in the music of the moment. He really did his best thinking at times like that.

"Swing" by Sophie Tucker

"Searching" by Change

"Lost In Yesterday" by Tame Impala

Saturday morning, the playlist began soft, with songs new and old and kinda sexy. Toni hoped to convey a little swing, sway and soul as he opened his shutters for fresh air and perhaps, fresh intrigue. Toni was here for new clients to teach English to, but Toni was not opposed to new friends, either.

"Be Thankful for What You Got" by William Vaughn

"Across the Room" by Odesza

"Je Nous Aime" by Claude Challe

"Take Me to the Alley" by Gregory Porter

"Merula" by Lund Quartet

As the day picked up and the sun rose higher, Paloma came and went with errands and shopping, the music changing to things more bouncy, rhythmic and fun.

"Peaches" by Krafty Kuts

"Anyday" by Eric Clapton

"I Got You" by Duke Dumont

"As" by Stevie Wonder

Paloma found them all to be intriguing. Stirring even. She was tempted to knock on the door and introduce herself, driven as much by curiosity as her quietly-admitted loneliness. In the days that followed, the music ran the buffet from "La Vie En Rose" by Grace Jones; "Cohete" by Gerardo Frisina; "Don't Sweat the Technique" by Eric B. & Rakim; and the haunting "Steve Reich: Music for 18 Musicians". It was that rainy Sunday night that "Music for 18 Musicians", a veritable soundtrack to the rainstorm, that captivated her. It was unlike anything she had ever heard before and she was mesmerized and now fascinated by the man behind this music. She sat in the darkness of her apartment by the window, had three cigarettes from an old pack on the shelf she would indulge in on boozy nights and listened to both the rain and the music. She felt like she could actually float.

Toni was a man in equal measures simple and complex, straightforward and sweetly vague, cosmopolitan but never too trendy, which was too temporary for Toni, who tried to carry himself with a bit of timelessness and solidity. He was a genuine, authentic, caring warm and approachable man, unless someone wronged him in some way, and then he could be a surprisingly ferocious and unforgiving street fighter.

As he delightfully discovered, he was just like Paloma in so many respects.

Paloma was different in her own way, different from anyone else she ever knew and she kept those differences to herself – "...*No se pueden dar margaritas a los cerdos...*" she would think while smiling sweetly and falsely. Her father had taught her never to apologize for who she was in thought, word or deed, but to be polite as well as unwavering about her values and convictions. And yet, there was a secret ruthlessness to Paloma – she did not take anyone's shit, whether it was bad service at a restaurant or department store, bad bosses or colleagues at work or anyone who dared jump the line on which she was waiting patiently on. They all got Paloma's "business". And that included Carmen, the cold witch in apartment 3.

On Sunday, she had to instinctively stop herself from knocking on the door to ask La Senora if she wanted bread from the bakery –

they always offered two-for-one on Sundays - catching herself to realize someone new lived there now. But she also bit her lip on the way down the stairs, thinking *that* might be a dirty-but-delicious opening gambit – feigned ignorance always had a seductive air about it a few layers deep, depending on how many layers deep this new neighbor was stacked. And while private herself, she was just nosy enough to seriously think about it.

Turns out, she didn't have to – he would do it for them in the clumsiest, most adorable way the following day. Time would tell whether it was an accident or not.

Carmen

THE NEW NEIGHBORS' PRESENCE – she figured it had to be a 'him' by way of the cigar smoke signals he was sending one flight up - made no difference to Carmen. Its occurrence meant nothing: nothing new, nothing different, no reason to think or wonder. Carmen was not a very curious person, as curiosity, her father had told her many times with her mother in silent and fearful agreement, brought trouble. Carmen had succumbed, by and large, to the numbness of her life and daily thoughts.

While sight unseen, they did share a one-flight-up-at-an-angle balcony to her apartment 3, which allowed her to listen to his musical choices via the open terrace shutters. As for music, his tastes *were* diverse. She found them different. Intriguing even. At worst, occasionally annoying; at best, fascinating. They even gave rise to some unusual inquisitiveness, wondering who the DJ behind this intoxicating mix was? "Exotic and different" were not in Carmen's general vocabulary.

Most of these songs, almost all of them really, were new to Carmen. Her life was not filled with "pop" music or really any music. It's not that she wasn't interested in music, but generally thought it wild and unbecoming. She did occasionally secretly dance in front of her bedroom mirror after watching kids dancing on a TV program she had stumbled upon. "Hmm that looks like fun" she shamefully admitted to herself, unsure exactly what "fun" truly was and try as she may, she could not dismiss the idea of imitating them like an old church lady might. But the mirror dancing, after making sure the curtains were drawn low and tight, confirmed her fears of her own clumsiness, awkwardness and simple uncool-ness. The nerd in her was her - it defined all the other aspects of her, body and soul. She long accepted this sad reality, quietly and sometimes angrily.

Carmen "just was": opaque stockings, flat shoes for her aching feet, simple dark shift dresses and unremarkable clothes to fit loosely on her slender and unremarkable though not entirely unsexy body (Toni would think "tits on a stick" and smile to himself after meeting Carmen for the first time.) "Nothing to see here, move along..." was generally her attitude with men. Straight hair, tight non-smile, a state of perpetual (public) caution, wariness and coldness. A semi-present sneer that some might call a scowl. And she rather liked it that way – no one bothered Carmen, for pretty much any reason, be it a catcall or something more friendly, like asking for directions. She radiated unapproachability. This was her secret dominant side, which ran shockingly deep even for her.

It's been said we all have three lives: the public one...the private one...and the secret one. Carmen had a heaping portion of the secret one.

And yet, in some women who are neither beautiful nor pleasant as others, there is an invincible charm that attracts men and makes other women who cannot see it disdainful, because it acts only on men. The reason is that a certain woman is more woman than another is the same reason as between two bottles of wine of the same size: one contains more aroma and essence of wine than another, so in a woman there is much more femininity in one than in another.

(DIFFERENT ANONYMOUS INTERNET PHILOSOPHER)

Unbeknownst to her, apartment 2 had moved in earlier that week with few possessions beyond three suitcases and during a day for her that had stretched long into the Barcelona evening of dull work, customers, tourists and of course, no one to have an after-work drink and tapa with, except herself at the kitchen table, with a bottle of gin. Carmen usually passed on the tonic. And the tapa.

She fought the urge - natural for most, oddly disquieting for her - to lean around the edge of the shutter…to peek through the keyhole… to listen in the staircase for the keys in his door one flight down and "accidently" create the hallway moment of "Oh! Hello, you must be the new neighbor!"

Though some men do, not everyone loves difficult, angular, almost inaccessible women. Only apparently are they sunny and outgoing, even self-confident, but in reality they are always wary, insecure and always on the defensive. And they keep everything inside. Don't look them too much in the eye, because they don't want anyone to see their anger, disappointment, fear or fragility. Loneliness accompanies them, even when they have dozens of suitors. Because they love but they never depend on love, on that love that is only a dream for them. And they are hard, first of all on themselves. Only those who know how to look "beyond" the smile can see the impenetrable wall they have erected. Who defends their rich but wounded, frightened interiority. Their sensitivity hurt too many times. The difficult experience that only they know. Because they are angular, difficult women.

(SOME OTHER ANONYMOUS INTERNET PHILOSOPHER)

On Sunday, Carmen went to church, because, well, Carmen went to church, without much thought or care, but with guilt and mind-numbing regularity. Carmen never actually found God in church, but something came over her during communion that Sunday to try and "find" apartment 2 and Toni.

Senora Lopez's bakery had been in the neighborhood for many years, and it showed on her – hunched, slow and only with the rare/occasional smile. She was the older version of Carmen, in many ways. Her croissants, however, were a level above acceptable and on Sundays, her "*barra*" baguettes were always two-for-one. No rejecting the second one, ever, that's just how it was. Many a pigeon was fed by the second loaf when one proved to be more than sufficient.

A bag with a croissant and two loaves wrapped in paper, artfully twisted at the ends as only Europeans can do, under her arm, she went home with an undetectable but dirty grin on her face. Carmen was not going to wait to bump into apartment 2 or for that matter, let Paloma swoop in and get an early jump on things, just in case apartment 2 turned out to be…well, something interesting.

Paloma, to Carmen, was many things and everything that Carmen was not: pretty, successful by any standard, stylish and outwardly sophisticated. It irked Carmen to run into Paloma in the lobby, or worse, leave her apartment moments after Paloma did, finding herself surrounded by the last trailing whiffs of Paloma's always-delightful perfume lingering in the stairway. It put an immediate frown of self-judgement on Carmen's face. Every time. She almost thought to leave earlier than normal just to avoid the assault on her senses.

Tap! Tap! Tap! Carmen heard the music coming from Toni's apartment and hence figured he was home, though she did not knows the state of his dress or readiness to greet someone at the door. Her impertinent urgency took even her by surprise, but there had been many dark moments recently when she'd sat alone with her gin-sans-tonic and began to think and feel "enough is enough" about her unhappiness, her loneliness, her awkwardness. Although she'd been elevated to oversee the tellers at the BBVA bank on Via Laietana, her work was still brutally dull. And alone with her TV at night, watching programs of places she could never imagine actually visiting, or glumly watching the fools on "First Dates" actually have dates was becoming too much to bear. Even her forays into feminine domination pornography were less riveting as they had been in the past: the place to turn to was turning out to be tuning her out. There was no one to dominate.

So she summoned her long-lost (and minimally) sweet side, already "dressed in her Sunday best" (which was barely a notch about her Monday-to-Friday dress, but still) and listened for just a second across the hall at Paloma's apartment, hoping she would be either peeking through the door or listening behind it. The tap-tap-tap just might arouse her to the door and watch Carmen begin to squeeze her talons into Toni.

Toni answered the door, hoping, thinking, expecting it to be Paloma. "*Hola!* I am Carmen, your neighbor upstairs. Welcome to the building!" Carmen exclaimed as she eyed Toni up and down with a kind of dirty grin. Hmm! thought Carmen, so young and fresh-looking is this boy!

"Oh *hola!* I am Toni. Nice to meet you – Oh sorry, am I making too much noise already?" Toni stammered a bit, taken aback by this Sunday morning visit, though fortunately he was dressed and ready for the day. Carmen radiated a false smile, her eyes darting behind Toni to peek inside his place.

"No, no not at all! I find your music very….interesting!" Carmen just could not be Carmen and lie straight-faced. Her forced smiled immediately outed her. "Here, I brought you a little something for your Sunday breakfast – as you may know most stores and restaurants are closed today and the bakery offers two-for-one on Sundays – it's very fresh!"

"Oh why thank you very much. It's very kind of you!" Toni said, warily smiling back at Carmen's insincere grin.

"Well, welcome again to the building – let me know if you need anything. "Anything at all" she seductively (for Carmen) murmured. I'm right upstairs."

"Yes thanks again" said Toni, waving his baton of bread as a farewell. Toni thought "Hmm now I've met my two neighbors. Clearly there will be only one winner in this race, but this might be interesting!"

The devil in Toni sensed, in time, he could get whatever he wanted from Paloma and take whatever he wanted from Carmen. But while the thought of this juggling act of selfish whoring crossed his mind, in the same moment, he "felt" the power of Paloma upon him and chose not to mess up what just might be the best thing of his life.

Toni began to embrace, more and more, the Spanish rhythm of the day – early (and many throughout-the-day) coffee; midday snack; late (by his standards) lunch; an after work *tapa*; and dinner at 9.30. His life also took on a rhythm, preparing lesson plans and teaching; his delightful, unencumbered cigar smoking; his music and trying (poorly) to cook for himself. Lastly, he slipped comfortably into the comings-and-goings of his building: he soon could tell by the clip-clop of their shoes who was walking up or down the stairs as each had a distinctive cadence to their steps: Senora Pinasa had the hard deter-mination of a woman going somewhere directly with no time to waste. Carmen's was softer, flatter, duller, more of a kind of soft-shoe scrape. Paloma's was a strong, forceful, confident stiletto-strut. If Toni had had a foot fetish, this would be thrilling! It was forty-five steps from the front door to Toni's apartment, two steps apart from Paloma's. It was twenty-three more up to Carmen's. He loved the sound of Paloma strut. He came to dread the approaching sound of Carmen's.

Paloma had tried to make friends with Carmen a year or so earlier – another neighbor on the fourth floor, the lovely Senora Pinasa, had mentioned to Paloma while sorting through the mail in the lobby "Dios mio, what wonderful cooking and especially baking smells come from your apartment, Paloma!" She told Carmen that soon after she mentioned it to Paloma, Paloma knocked on her door with an apple tart! Paloma had, at times, baked something sweet for her father and Marta and made an extra portion of whatever she was cooking for La Senora across the hall, so she thought it would be a nice thing to do for Senora Pinasa since she complemented her on the aromas of her cooking. And it *was* delicious, Senora Pinasa exclaimed!

Though Carmen worked hard at avoiding Paloma and her general fabulousness, one day Carmen ran into her at an odd hour for both of them at the mail station and, curious in an evil kind of Carmen-way, also mentioned the enticing aroma often coming from Paloma's apartment. Carmen was nice only to get something in life, and never actually praised someone or something. She never had taken the time to write an online review of anything, and definitely not a positive one, except for porn she liked on Porn Hub, anonymously, of course. But she wanted to try this (supposedly) super-duper apple tart. Why should Senora Pinasa have all the fun and goodies? So she fawned, through slightly gritted teeth, about the smells of such goodness emanating from apartment 1, hoping for a slice so she could, most probably, sniff in derision at it all in the privacy of apartment 3.

As it happened, it *was very good*, she silently admitted to herself. Damn this woman, is she average at *anything*, Carmen fumed? She ran into Paloma about a week after receiving the tart. "Oh it was delicious – just a bit too sweet for me, but very, very enjoyable, thank you!" That was Carmen at her kindest, a backhanded slap at the gift giver and a week later, no less. Paloma returned the gritted grin with a kind a growl and a guttural "Oh you're welcome, though no one ever complained about my tart before. Maybe I can adjust the recipe to suit you better next time" said Paloma with visions of ground-glass sprinkled like confectioners' sugar over the crust.

Two weeks later on a Friday night, Carmen the cashier supervisor realized she needed to run to the bank ATM on the corner. She'd normally never go out at that late hour but needed money to pay for a package she expected to be delivered early the next morning – some sex toys and femme domination DVD's. Carmen had not graduated her technology, or her life, or wardrobe, or pretty much anything about herself, as evidenced by her reliance on DVD's and her perfectly good flip-phone.

As she scraped down the stairs, she not only smelled something delicious, but heard laughing and music coming from Paloma's apartment – it was Toni and Paloma on a dinner date, and she quietly flew into a rage! She was a poor cook so she could not offer Toni any kind of treats as Paloma did, or apparently had been. In fact, she could not offer Toni much of anything, except, well, what?

Paloma and Carmen's positions had both formed and hardened over the year, though, oddly, very little was said or exchanged between them. Carmen always had a look on her face somewhere between perpetually annoyed and bitter resignation at her lot in life, self-imposed as it were. And Paloma was simply too busy and too pretty to be concerned with a pouty neighbor who actually dismissed her apple tart! So a kind of silent truce was put in place: no war, but no peace, either. And that snap about her apple tart stung Paloma, a burr that would not be easily buffed away.

They avoided each other as best as they could. They snooped at each other's mail. Paloma waited for church to begin before getting bread for her and Toni, who did not really want it but loved the gesture and Paloma at his door with a sweet gift. Carmen slogged her way past apartment 1 on her way up and down the stairs. Détente was in place. But there was also an unknown but silently shared and growing angst developing in apartment 1 and apartment 3 – loneliness and frustration, the only two things Carmen and Paloma would share, until Toni came along.

Carmen's mother had passed away a few years earlier. She'd done the best she could with her, but with few examples of love and caring in her life, her help was often routine and perfunctory. Instead of feeling like the shackles of nearly twenty-four years of off-and-on care had been broken, Carmen, not knowing any other way to live, stayed dark and quiet and withdrawn. She did not feel free and book a month-long cruise or fly to the US and visit New York and Washington DC and California as she had imagined she might. Nothing much changed, in reality – Carmen simply did not know any other way to live.

Paloma's father Nacho had passed peacefully about nine months before, Paloma was crushed but happy that Nacho had lived a truly long and full life and died peacefully in his own home. Paloma, unlike Carmen, felt lifted and unleashed, not that Nacho was a burden, not at all. But now it was just her in this world, no siblings or parents, so she threw herself into work and even scanned Tinder on the weekends for the secret thrill of the acknowledgment, though she was turned off by 99 percent of all possible inquiries. The dick pic's, however, were occasionally stirring!

Enter Toni, and Paloma's entire world changed.

Toni was all Paloma sought in a man, in love, companionship and overall, a relationship. She sometimes was as in love with the possession of such a man as she was in love with the man himself.

Carmen's version of unburdening herself was to grow darker – she felt unwatched and unjudged for the first time in her life and dove into that which intrigued her on a disturbing level: feminine domination pornography. Watching it fed the ever-present sense of worthlessness she had always felt by allowing her a sense of control and revenge. She saw a report on television about it and with no one looking over her shoulder, began to investigate and thrill herself in a manner she'd never known before. She also delved online, but it wasn't Tinder: it was Fetlife.com.

Sant Jordi

APRIL 23RD IS SANT JORDI DAY in Catalunya. It is a kind of Valentine's Day, with men giving roses to their special ladies and ladies giving a book in return. The holiday honors San Jordi, a knight who slayed the dragon that was terrorizing towns in Catalunya moments before the dragon could kill the fair princess. Where the blood of the dragon soaked the ground, a rosebush blossomed and Jordi gave a rose to the princess.

For both men and women, the day is met with happiness and not the dread of being rejected or heartbroken. The streets of Barcelona are thronged with flower stalls and long racks of books. Toni got the lowdown on Sant Jordi protocol from a few of his students the weekend before and began to scout florist locations and consider the timing of giving Paloma a rose. Or perhaps more than one rose.

Toni and Paloma, from the first accidental bump, lit a fuse for one another that had long been cold, wet and dormant for both. They genuinely enjoyed each other's company and helped each other with their language skills – she got free English lessons and he learned more Catalan than he ever imagined he could. She was also, as the building's residents knew, a fabulous cook (unlike Toni and his three-times-per-week omelet dinners) and he was a warm, funny man with great taste in music. Toni was simply fun and charming company for anyone, but especially Paloma. In very short order, she found herself not just enjoying the idea of a boyfriend, but falling truly, deeply in love with Toni. As happy and as successful as her life was, Paloma was crushingly bored and lonely, though she did a very good at hiding it publicly. Now that she had found Toni, and Toni, her, she fully and completely embraced "them" declaring to herself to do everything in her power to make them unbreakable.

Everything.

Carmen understood what was going on downstairs and she was none too happy about. In fact, as she painfully came to know, whenever "Ravel's Bolero" would waft through the apartment shutters, Carmen was triggered to head straight to the gin; the grunting and banging and shouts of orgasmic pleasure were soon to follow and Carmen was *not* interested in voyeurism, but action all for herself. Paloma could not have been more thrilled, especially when she "caught" Carmen attempting to flirt with him in the lobby one afternoon. It was both humorous and deliciously evil to know that Carmen was pressing the issue and yet Toni was quietly in her bed many times during the week. Although 11, Carrer de l'Argenteria and its fancy scrollwork front door was built in 1786, its walls were not as thick as one might imagine (and the plumbing was another story all to itself.) So while Paloma wanted to make noise in every way she could, knowing the power of its upward drift towards apartment 3, Toni urged restraint even during the many explosive moments in each other's bed, for fear of inciting the neighbor(s).

For Paloma, Toni was heaven-sent in every way. For Carmen, Toni was a life and a person and an experience far out of reach, though she ached to change that and thought Sant Jordi would be the perfect opportunity to lure Paloma away.

Loneliness was a kind of hex. Carmen resented Paloma. Paloma reveled in her newfound love *and* her superiority over Carmen. But Carmen was not going to take being dismissed lying down or with a shrug, like she did everything else in her boring life.

Toni was always polite when he bumped into Carmen, though he knew he had a pained smile that looked well beyond the conversation to other places he'd rather be at that moment. Carmen wore the face of early alcoholism, with slightly rheumy eyes and blotched, vein-destroying skin and Toni could not look past that, though he tried. When he saw her smoking in front of the building, she took loooong drags, to deepen her thoughts and misery. Without the cooking skills of Paloma, Carmen turned to myth and legend in the hopes of making herself more desirable and clear to Toni of her intrigue with him. She spent the Saturday before Sant Jordi looking for the right book to give him, hoping she would receive a rose from Toni and her life would be changed, perhaps forever.

She found "The Shadow of the Wind" a book about the mysterious aftermath of the Spanish Civil War. It was dark, which Carmen increasingly was and sexy, which Carmen was not. Inside the book, she also slipped her business card, and on the back of her card, a move of shocking audacity, she wrote the URL of her three very favorite porn clips, to make sure Toni understood what was available to him. It was not a cake, or dinner, like Paloma offered, but it was, or could be, Carmen. But with nothing to offer and less than nothing to lose, Carmen went for broke – she was already broken.

Carmen understood intensely what was going on one flight down. Not every shout was muffled; the banging of the headboard, the lamp on the side table crashing to the floor, the post-orgasm cigarettes on the terrace. Carmen understood, which, as an odd side benefit, aided her own fantasies alone in her bed. Carmen thought "Well, two can play at this game – I can't get to a man's heart through his stomach, but maybe I can get there between my legs?"

Carmen rang Toni's bell early in the day as the city was waking to Sant Jordi, hoping to get a jump on what Paloma was surely planning. No one answered her knock at the door. Well, not directly: Toni was, in fact, across the hall, and when he heard the knock, he peeked through Paloma's keyhole to see who it was. Heart racing and naked, he put his finger to both his lips and Paloma's to stifle their laughter.

He liked Paloma, very much, but also was not cruel and did not want any trouble over his head.

Carmen debated whether to leave the book on his doorstep, but decided the in-person presentation would have more impact. Kind of a waste of eye-shadow, she thought, as she re-buttoned the top of her blouse, but I will catch him later.

Paloma immediately traded her smirk for her outrage. *Hija de puta*, Paloma fumed, how *dare* that Carmen! Carmen had seen her and Toni holding hands in the street, in the Casa Pisco bar next door and once in the Mercat de Santa Caterina clearly buying things for a dinner *together*. And yet, thought Paloma, she dismissed the obvious "thing" she and Toni had going on and made her Sant Jordi play anyway. Remember that ruthless side of Paloma? Carmen was about to be reminded of it.

Toni slipped out of Paloma's apartment to wash up and get changed for the day. He took a quick walk to the florist in the nearby Passatge Sert and found a few beautiful rose displays, wrapped in Catalan flag ribbons and decorated with symbolic lavender and baby's breath. He did, as a peace offering, consider buying a rose for Carmen, but quickly imagined setting fire to Paloma and the fantastic relationship they had developed, and thought (much) better of it. *Que sera sera*, he thought, Paloma is my girl!

On the way back to the apartment, who did he pass with his rose bouquet but Carmen coming down the steps? Uh oh, he thought, trapped in the stairwell just below the landing for apartments 1 and 2. "Good morning Carmen! Happy Sant Jordi to you!"

"Oh hello Toni, to you as well! Oh I see you have some lovely roses there!" as she lowered he head to take the book for Toni from her bag. Toni gulped, blushed and stammered all at once. "Here, this is for you!" exclaimed Carmen, on the verge of the place between tears, heartbreak and the immediate need for more gin at home.

"Oh, well, um, thank you so much" said Toni, slowly inching past Carmen to get to his door. "It's so kind of you and yes what a lovely day this seems to be. Well thanks again!" he said, rudely leaving a devastated and rose-less Carmen quickly on the landing while he rushed inside his door.

In the hallways of 11, Carrer de l'Argenteria, much was heard though little was said between the neighbors and don't you know Paloma had heard the entire exchange. She found herself giddy at the prospect of roses from Toni – her book with a scented spray of her favorite perfume along with a loving inscription in flowing calligraphy inside, was at the ready by the keys at the front door – and boiling mad at Carmen's insulting attempt to sabotage her relationship with Toni. She silently burned and could have left scorch marks on her ceramic tile floor if she did not have the happy knowledge that those roses in Toni's arms were for her and only her.

But that was not enough for Paloma. This attempted theft was going to stop. Very, very soon.

Le Tart Tatin

TONI AND PALOMA SILENTLY HOWLED with laughter and outrage when they visited Carmen's "favorite" porn links. After eyebrows were raised and the color returned to their faces, they began to plan a weekend away. Their time together had grown better and stronger, learning and experiencing things they had only dreamed of in a partner and Paloma was determined to allow *nothing and no one* to mess with this paradise she had discovered in, of all places, the apartment right across the hall from all her loneliness.

Carmen, sadly, faced her cold reality with a level of pain and resignation she had not felt in a very long time. When Toni, without a rose for Carmen, obviously and quickly said goodbye, Carmen felt stupid and horrified and furious and crushingly sad all at once and all the revenge porn on the internet could not put her in a good place. Paloma, behind the door, felt the exact opposite of each of Carmen's emotions, and Carmen knew it, adding to her pain.

She had bared her soul, and nearly her skin, to Toni, who brushed it aside with a countenance of shock and awkward near-disgust. Another bastard of a man would have taken Carmen up on her offer of madness and perversity, but Toni – good for him, bad for Carmen - was not that kind of man. He had already fallen deeply for Paloma and had zero interest in anyone or anything else that might compromise his very, very good thing with her.

It's moments like this that make people, many people, any and all people, to think dark, violent thoughts, about themselves and about their perceived transgressors. Carmen helplessly recognized the downward spiral she was spinning on. She went for broke and was left broken, exposed and humiliated. She did not blame Toni, but a bit of herself and even though it made no sense, she blamed Paloma too, for being all the things Carmen was not. Though true before, now it was crystal clear: Paloma was Toni's girlfriend, another thing Carmen would never be.

Immersed in misery, the thought crossed back and forth and back again that Paloma should die – if Carmen couldn't have Toni, or transform herself into anything that resembled a happy, sexy, fun, clever, talented person like Paloma, then neither could Paloma. But how? Of course it made no sense, but what does when you are consuming yourself in gin, deviant pornography, misery and jealousy? Rolling up the rugs and stomping around her apartment making noise in heavy dominatrix boots above Paloma seemed to fall short of the satisfaction of murder to Carmen. She poured another glass and parked herself in front of the TV to watch her favorite brutalizing porn star, Cherry

Torn. She slipped a DVD of hers into the player as she slipped in and out of conscious sanity.

The thought of killing Paloma dissolved over the ice cubes in her gin. But in apartment 1, the thought of killing Carmen bubbled hot like a pie in Paloma's oven.

Paloma ran into Carmen a few days later and thought to misdirect her intentions by playing extra nice. "Oh hi Carmen! *Como estas?*" "*Bien*" mumbled Carmen, obviously wearing her recent rendezvous with alcohol on her tired, bloodshot face.

"I see you and the new neighbor are getting along nicely, aren't you?" growled Carmen, making no effort to hide her fury and sadness.

"Yes, he is a very sweet man and we are enjoying the springtime together very much." Paloma smiled through an evil, malicious grin, making no effort to hide her superior happiness. "Hey, I was thinking about your comment that my apple tart was too sweet for you and I adjusted the recipe. Would you like to try my new adaptation? I think it's turned out very well."

Carmen, so miserable and defeated following her Sant Jordi Day catastrophe, found herself agreeing to the idea of kindness from her enemy, a Trojan horse about to gallop into apartment 3. "Sure, why not? Maybe this weekend you can drop it off? I don't have any plans so I should be home" Carmen glumly admitted to both of them.

"OK great, I'll do that! Well, I have to run and get ready. Toni and I are going out for a fancy dinner to celebrate our 3 month anniversary. I will see you soon though" said Paloma cheerfully, turning the knife clockwise and then back again for added emphasis.

Recipe for Tarte Tatin Paloma-style

- 225g store bought puff pastry
- 10 large apples, either Braeburn or Granny Smith, peeled and halved or quartered
- Juice of 1 ripe lemon
- 110g butter roughly chopped
- 45g caster sugar
- A shake of ground cinnamon
- A **big pinch** of ground cloves and nutmeg

1. Preheat the oven to 200°C.

2. Pack the apples into a large frying pan with a metal handle, presentation side down. Pack the apples tightly because they shrink during cooking.

3. Dot the apples with butter, sprinkle on the sugar and spices.

4. Place the pan onto the heat and shake gently while the butter and sugar caramelize.

5. Splash on the juice of 1 lemon, this adds pectin and thickens the caramel; Do not brown the caramel too much.

6. Simmer gently for about five –ten minutes and then let the apples cool down.

7. Lightly flour a cool surface and roll out the pastry about 5mm thick.

8. Cut a circle to fit the top of the pan.

9. Place the pastry on top of the apples and tuck it around them. Make a few little slits in the pastry to allow the steam to escape,

10. Bake the tart for 25-to-30 minutes or until the pastry is golden and the filling is bubbling.

11. Remove the tart from the oven and let it cool for 10-15 minutes.

12. When you are ready to serve the tart run a knife around the edge of the pan to loosen the pastry.

13. Cover with a plate large enough to cover the tart and holding them both tightly, invert the pan and plate to remove the tart.

Paloma smiled a filthy smile when the time came for the "pinch" of nutmeg and cloves. "A bit too sweet, eh?" she thought, equally furious and wickedly delighted to turn the tables on Carmen. She grated a fistful of nutmeg into a small bowl along with the clove pieces. "I'll show her not to mess with me! Give *my* man a book and your dirty fantasies, will you?"

In an earlier life, Paloma was a pastry chef (or thought she wanted to be) and as part of her training, learned that ingesting too much nutmeg or too much clove could be fatal. Cloves contained eugenol, a highly-complex chemical that is used in a variety of ways in many different products. Excessive amounts would cause seizures and shock, disrupting the brains electrical activity and causing anaphylaxis. Throw in an increased risk of bleeding, vomiting and numbness as well as a sudden drop in blood sugar and the coma it could induce if not quickly reversed. Thought the apples were naturally sweet, there was little added sugar to offset this potential. She was not going to make it even a single grain sweeter for Carmen!

As for the nutmeg, one to two tablespoons would cause arrhythmia, nausea and vomiting, angst, paranoia, dry mouth and severe hallucinations. Its detection could also be masked by extra dairy in a recipe.

Cloves and nutmeg were also very hard to detect in an autopsy. Hector, Paloma's old boyfriend, was a police detective who had jokingly mentioned that early in their relationship after he had a slice of her apple tart. Besides, she had access to some of the best lawyers in Barcelona.

Paloma had overheard Carmen telling Senora Pinasa that she was "slightly diabetic" – lonely people often have the habit of over-sharing. At any moment. Anywhere. What she didn't mention, as they chatted in the hallway, was that the many empty bottles of gin clanking in her garbage bag were not helping her condition. The alcohol alone could be the cause of her demise – it would be the river to her veins of the deadly-delicious apple tart.

Paloma wanted to bide her time, waiting for the right cultural moment to present Carmen with her "new and improved" recipe. But the Festival of Merce, the patron saint of Barcelona honoring "Our Lady of Mercy" did not occur until the end of the summer. Paloma could not wait until then as her anger and resentment of Carmen, as well as her growing affection for Toni, were locking themselves into place. Both relationships had become unbreakable, one of love and one of hate.

More and more the moments of her conviction to knock Carmen off outweighed the insanity of the idea itself, but her love for Toni had made her blind to the very possible consequences. She had ached for so long for love, true love, and now that it was here – only two steps away – she became even more fervent in her desire to hold onto it and never let it go, no matter how hard someone, anyone, tried to pry it loose from her.

The recipe was easy to plan, though she could never actually taste the results. The smell alone told her she was in the zone of deliciousness and would be free of any suspicion, beyond the inherent dislike between the two.

At this point, Paloma had all five corners of her deadly pentagram covered:

Who: Carmen.

What: deadly apple tart.

Where: apartment 3

Why: Toni

Now for the "when":

July 16! Santa Maria Del Carmen! Mother of God, it was Carmen's "name" day in honor of Saint Carmen, who protects all seafaring people. Saint Peter might be special to fishermen but Carmen looks after all who use the sea in any capacity. Ships of all kinds, festooned with lights, flowers and ornaments are blessed in the harbor. Well, Carmen will be sleeping with the fishes very soon, thought Paloma, amusing herself in a diabolical way that felt perfectly normal.

All the ingredients were in place. The lovemaking with Toni took on a special urgency and intensity in the days and weeks leading up to July 16. Paloma's deepening commitment to Toni mesmerized him even further and also threw him off the scent of what Paloma was planning.

Carmen caught Paloma leaving a bit late for work one day about a week before the planned tart delivery and commented on the aromas emanating from apartment 1. "Yes Carmen, I am testing variations of my recipe to suit your low sugar taste preference. Who doesn't like sweet things?" Paloma taunted her crabby, sour neighbor. "But its ok. Perhaps you have a condition? Well, I think I am just about ready to present my tart to you – it will be soon. Hey, maybe I can have it ready for your Saints Day? I had an Aunt Carmen so I know it's coming up on the 16th, right?"

"Um, yes, well its very kind of you, really, to make this effort, Paloma" said Carmen warily, her antennae raised on two counts: first it *was* Paloma, her building arch-enemy and then, hmm she seemed so cheerful at the prospect of giving Carmen a gift, hand- made no less. No one did that for Carmen. But, well, it did also feel nice to have someone offer a kind word and even a gift, for once, so Carmen smiled back, *somewhat* sincerely – it *was* Carmen, after all – and said "Thank you again. Yes I expect to be home all weekend. Except for church on Sunday, of course."

"Okay then, I'll see you just as soon as the recipe turns out perfectly. I would not want to give you anything but my very best. *Adeu* Carmen!"

Paloma was wound tight with excitement and it showed during Friday night's love making session with Toni. It got dirty, heated, oiled and filled with scratches and caresses, fueled not only by the delicious cava Toni brought, but by the excitement about her plan. The only thing Paloma could taste besides Toni was victory over Carmen.

Paloma wore Toni out by design Friday night and he slept through her tart baking Saturday morning. Bzzzzz! Paloma put on her favorite perfume, best heels and tight jeans to present Carmen with her Saints Day apple tart – she wanted to knock her out right at the door and leave her scent lingering in Carmen's entry.

"*Bon dia* Carmen! Happy Saints Day!" Paloma wickedly exclaimed. Carmen, slowly recovering again from too much gin and not enough of anything else, could not have looked less like Paloma, and Paloma knew her timing, as such, would be impeccable. "Oh *hola* Paloma" Carmen half grumbled. "Oh yes, the apple tart!" Carmen, still slightly grumpy, perked up at the thought that this had been made just for her! How nice! With any and all suspicions out the third floor window in the face of such an odd occurrence, she happily accepted the tart.

"Thank you very much! I am sure it will be absolutely delicious. It's so kind of you."

"Well, it *is* your Saints Day, so I hope you enjoy it. I bet you'll like it so much you can eat it the whole thing in a day or two! I think a big scoop of vanilla ice cream would go great with it! Enjoy!" And with that, Paloma shut the door on Carmen forever, she hoped.

Using latex gloves, Paloma had placed the tart in a simple aluminum pie pan and then put it in a plain brown bag. She covered the tart with tin foil.

Carmen was immediately delighted with the gift, but at that hour, with her head pounding, she was in no mood for something sweet, even something less-sweet-than-usual. So she set the tart on her kitchen table, peeked under the foil Paloma had covered it with, actually smiled and then went back to bed, leaving the tart untouched.

Paloma headed straight to Toni's apartment, feeling triumphant that phase one was now complete. She quietly slipped into apartment 2 using the set of keys Toni had given her and slithered under the blankets to wake up Toni in a *very* special way. Carmen had gotten something deadly for her mouth and now Paloma was getting something delicious for hers!

On Saturday night, with all the laundry done and the house cleaned, Carmen spun through her pornography collection and came upon a new favorite porn star, Isis Love. She snuggled in for a deep dive of her ball-cracking mayhem and a big goblet of gin.

Smiling a filthy grin at some of the previews, Carmen remembered the apple tart and decided it was the perfect time to try it along with, in honor of her Saints Day, a large scoop of vanilla ice cream on top.

She warmed a big slice in the toaster oven and set the ice cream container on top of it to soften some for her treat. The bell dinged and out came a warm, oh-so-fragrant slice of what she thought was a sweet gift from her sour neighbor. The smell was heavenly, so aromatic with nutmeg and cinnamon and, oh clove too! Well, this was going to be delicious!

Pre-soused, Carmen dug in. Well, well it *was* indeed not too sweet! A borderline diabetic, she thought, hmmm I could have *two slices* and still be good!

Yum-yumming her way through the tart, the ice cream and Isis Love, Carmen found herself actually happy for about thirty minutes of food porn and real porn, until the chaos of both began to take effect.

Slowly but surely, Carmen had a creeping sensation of dizzy nervousness, as if the tart had super doses of caffeine. She soon began to feel wild-eyed and paranoid, quickly jumping from the bed, tripping over an empty bottle of gin at her bedside, to pull the drapes tight, even tighter than they already were.

Suddenly she began gasping, wheezing. Oh no, oh no she thought, did I have too much gin and maybe the apples are not mixing well with it? Fuck, life was fine forty minutes ago! Or? Or?

She became more scared, more sick, more nervous, more dizzy and more hallucinatory with each passing minute. The porn on the TV became almost lifelike and the screams of Isis Love's lovers were deafeningly loud and seemingly "real." She started shouting "I'm sorry, I'm sorry" at the TV while trying to get herself organized enough to crawl to the bathroom. It must be the gin, she kept thinking, never imagining a simple apple tart could make her feel this way.

But Carmen did not get all that far. While the tart began at working full-speed, Carmen slowed to less than a crawl and laid motionless on the floor between her bedroom and bathroom, on the two-step rise between them. She could not even feel the pain of the stair jabbing into her ribs. Cross-eyed and wheezing, she began flailing for something to grab, to give her the ability to lift herself and crawl to the toilet around the glass wall.

Paloma had planned an elegant evening at the Mandarin Oriental hotel followed by a long five-day weekend in France. She had arranged to rent a sexy red Audi R8 to drive to Carcassonne, Bergerac and Pau. They drank and ate and laughed and kissed and smirked and reveled in each other like neither ever had before. Paloma then suggested they go to the rooftop bar after their *cortado's* for a late nightcap just as the last of the sunset dipped over the western Mediterranean sky. They wrapped themselves around each other while toasting with the best cava on the menu. Their hearts and stomachs were full and giddy and they literally stumbled back to their room to sleep off the night and head to France early the next day.

Carmen, in her final gasping moments, was now paralyzed and beyond consciousness, unable to move or speak or cry for help. If this was Paloma's idea of a Friday night, "…a night with a personality…", well.

Delia, the cheerful Bolivian woman who came to the building every Monday morning to clean the entrance hall, lobby and stairway, stopped Senora Pinasa as she was returning to her apartment and asked if she had seen Carmen that week. "No actually, I have not but I have been busy packing for my trip. I am going to see my daughter in Chicago next week so I have been preoccupied with packing and preparing gifts to bring. Why do you ask?"

"Because this building *always* has lovely smells in the hallway. It's always such a treat! But today I smelled something terrible coming from Carmen's place."

"Qu'est-ce que tu as fait?"

TONI, IN HIS DRIVING CAP and sunglasses and Paloma with her scarf trailing in the wind, looked to be the perfect couple in love. Toni packed his Spotify playlist with songs that made them feel like soaring over the blacktop of the AP7, the A61 and the A65.

"It Aint Me" by Kygo & Selena Gomez

"Fetch Your Life" by Prince Kaybee

"Free" by Sault

And even an oldie-but-goodie from disco days, the singalong "Gypsy Woman" by Crystal Waters.

The weekend was pure bliss for them both – driving in the sunshine in the Audi, including a stick shift for Toni to enjoy – eating, drinking, fucking and even a bit of antiquing. If you didn't know better, you'd guess they were on their honeymoon, but Paloma knew better, and knew much more than Toni at that point. But their "disguise", and Toni's complete shock, was met with Gallic disbelief by the French National Gendarmerie in Pau.

When the National Police car passed Toni and then pulled in front of him, he didn't really think twice about it. He looked at the speedometer quickly and though he did not actually know the speed limit, many a Peugeot and Renault had already passed him that day. He did sit up a bit straighter when he saw another police car in his rear view mirror.

"Uh oh, was I going too fast? Toni quickly asked Paloma, who was watching both the GPS and some stupid cat videos on her phone. What is the speed limit, do you know?"

"No, but…." Paloma hesitatingly replied as the police car in front slowed and a second police car that suddenly arrived behind them turned its flashing lights on, boxing Toni in and forcing him to slow and follow the police car off the exit.

Both their faces flushed red, Toni's with confusion and Paloma's with complete but silent comprehension. The officer in the first car got out and approached Toni, hand on his gun, ominously. The other officer stayed in his vehicle while his partner approached the car on the passenger side, stopping to peek into the back seat and then down at Paloma's legs in her short skirt.

The first officer brought a small book with plasticized pages and flipped to a Spanish translation of "License, national identify card and registration please". Nervously, Toni leaned into Paloma and asked her "What does this say? What does he want?"

When the officer heard Toni speak English, he flipped the page to the one with the British flag and pointed to the translation.

Fumbling and stumbling but probably never more innocent of anything in his life, Toni fished out his documents while the passenger side officer tapped on the window and motioned for Paloma to open the door and get out.

While his head was turned to the first officer, hands shaking and trying hard to quickly calculate how fast in kilometers-per-hour he was going, he heard Paloma give a small shout. Toni turned his head to see her pressed up against the window being handcuffed.

"Wait, Monsieur, what is happening? What is the problem, *s'il vous plait*?" he asked in his not-very-good-French."

"*Demande à ta copine ! Vous êtes tous les deux en état d'arrestation. Merci de me donner vos clés.*" ("Ask your girlfriend! You're both under arrest. Please give me your keys.")

"What? *Que pasa?* Paloma!" Toni shouted as she was led, silently, to the backseat of the trailing police car while the first officer gave the keys to the Audi to his partner to follow to the gendarmerie.

"Toni! I'm sorry! Toni, *por favor, por favor!*" Paloma began crying with Toni in a state of complete astonishment and confusion. He immediately began to resist his arrest but stopped when he saw Paloma was not hysterical with confusion but instead, sobbing and compliant.

"What the fuck is happening? Paloma!" Toni screamed as he was put in the back of the first car.

Paloma knew there was no such thing as the perfect crime - she saw it every day in her law firm. Carmen knew there was no such thing as a "free lunch", or apple tart, as it were, and to never, ever trust the gift giver. Her cold life had painfully taught her that: she was rarely either the receiver or giver of gifts of any kind.

When Delia mentioned the smell, Senora Pinasa called the police, and when they came to break down the door, she clasped her hand to her mouth and began to cry – her unimaginable fears were about to be realized. She knew there was bad blood between Carmen and Paloma, but could *this be possible?* She quickly ran down the flight of stairs to knock, pound, on Paloma's door. Then Toni's. No answer.

Heads and cries popped out from every apartment – Pedro, Carmen's next-door neighbor, openly wept. Even Herman the German, who had spent the last ten years (more off than on) renovating his top-floor flat, looked pale and stunned and forced his two crying kids quickly back into their apartment because they wanted to see why the police were one floor below. And police fascinate kids.

Front and center in Carmen's place was a letter on the kitchen table. Sitting between the salt shaker and pepper grinder, the envelope was in Carmen's handwriting and its contents would lead the police, Spanish and very soon, French, directly to Paloma. Before Carmen had taken the first bite, she scratched a note saying "This apple tart was baked by and given to me by Paloma Remedios Lopez y Abad of apartment 1, *edificio* 11, Carrer de l'Argenteria. She is a woman seemingly of elegance but, in reality, of pure evil."

They found Carmen lying at a grotesque angle on the floor between her bedroom and bathroom. Her eyes were locked open, staring up at an angle toward the TV, where a brutal display of Isis Love videos played over and over. Her face, usually seen with a crooked grin, was contorted rather spookily into an almost half-smile. On the floor behind her was a sticky trail of melted ice-cream and shards of apple tart on the ground, now covered with ants, next to two empty bottles of gin.

Carmen was dead. Toni was in both shock and custody. Paloma sat in a French jail cell, quietly smirking.

Love, the search for love and the failure at finding love does indeed do strange things to people. As delusional as it seemed to Paloma that she could get away with it all, Carmen, in her infinite negativity, knew that no good deed goes unpunished. As they were in 11, Carrer L'Argenteria, if Carmen's suspicions were correct, then they surely would also be neighbors in hell. In the end, Carmen did not "get" Toni. But neither did Paloma, and that made Carmen smirk too.

And Toni? A fool for love, he drove home after two days pleading his innocence and ignorance in multiple languages and passing three lie-detector tests. Mournful music he always imagined to be part of his funeral now played in a continuous loop from his mobile phone all the way back to Barcelona.

"Internal Flight" by Estas Tonne

Aghast and bewildered, he vowed to move to a brand new apartment building as soon as he could pack his things. Since his life did not fill three suitcases, it would not take him long.

The Torch

THE PADDED ENVELOPE WAS A BIT TORN and clearly had been rained upon. The oil company I was contracted with had graciously paid the additional postage and forwarded it to me on the platform for the weekly mail-call. I opened it with a mixture of dread, trepidation, intrigue, curiosity and an unnerving micro-burst of possibilities and scenarios. I was torn between "Hmmm what could *this* be?" and "Uh-oh, could this *be*?"

I knew that handwriting immediately, from the curlicue "M" of "Mr. Nat Carlisle" on the address to the slight smudge his writing often left due to his advanced age, the series of mini-strokes he had experienced and the inherent, preternatural flourish to all he did.

My grandfather was sick and the twilight of his days was upon us all. I had been traveling for months at a time to places far from home with my job as a geologist so I didn't see much of him. He never really took to email, and barely a cell phone, which was rarely turned on anyway. We tried for some time to get him in front of an old but functioning computer to continue to electronically spin his lovely, sagacious tales and memories without the loss of imagination or clarity. He, however, felt the pen was infinitely mightier than the keyboard. As I slipped my finger through the gummy seal, I smiled sadly at what I feared above all else would be inside: his last letter to me. But you don't use a padded envelope for a letter.

I unfolded the paper, yellowed and creased as if it had been ironed by a tailor, but in reality, it was just GeBa Peday (which is what I'd called Grandpa Petey as a little boy, a moniker that stuck sweetly with the family all these years) using up the reams of old and yellowed stock he had neatly stacked in the cabinet along with the port wine glasses, the lace doilies no longer adorning the edges of the couch arms and the crystal decanter that held some wicked amber nectar that smelled like paint thinner and tasted like syrup of Ipecac.

"Dear Nat", he wrote, the letters D and N in sweeping calligraphic swirls as if copied from the Book of Kells, "The time has come to pass the torch, as it were, to you". Ah, "the torch". Swallowing hard, with my guts rising to the back of my throat, I laid the paper down like a newborn baby, lest I disturb a single syllable, and re-opened the envelope. Inside was GeBa's monogrammed handkerchief wrapped around "the torch": a mother-of-pearl fountain pen with the filigreed sterling silver "lace" accents on the crown, a Festinger 16mm,14k nib, ("…the Stradivarius of nibs, my boy…" he would exclaim) and a fresh pellet of the finest Sri Lankan ink, hand-stirred in a copper pot over coconut palms, derived from the livers of the purple-faced leaf monkeys of Indigo Island just off the coast of Colombo.

"My time has come, Nat, but yours is just beginning to see the rise of the sun. Take this and craft letters more beautiful than the women who will receive them. Write endlessly of your dreams and of your disparities, for they will surely come in some measure to balance your life and make you appreciate it all the more."

"Take this torch to illuminate the darker moments and to spread the light I've seen in you since the day you were born, a birthday we shared then, now and forever more. Write recipes and checks, write cards from strange places with even stranger rocks. Stain your fingers with its ink along with the wine which I hope often rests besides each letter you craft."

"I leave you this pen, Nat. It's not much as a solitary object. It sits there, still and motionless, until you pick it up, feel its weight, flip it between your fingers and let it scream with all the words yet to be written, all the possibilities and wisdom and anger and tumult and yes, still, love. I want you to have this before it becomes an object of lust and misplaced, ungainly familial desire, as the possessions of inheritance seem to be."

"Farewell Nat. Let this torch I cherished so much become a magic wand in your hand. Write declarations of peace and love, wonder, honesty and yes the occasional rebuke and retribution. Above all, let it be a baton that I now pass to you. My race is won, my race is done".